Death's Smile

By Nicki Lynn

Ink Smith Publishing

www.ink-smith.com

Death's Smile

Edited by Rachel Allcock & Corinne Anderson

Formatted by V.J.O. Gardner

Cover by Tatjana A.

Printed in the U.S.A

The final approval for this literary material is granted by the author.

ISBN: 978-1-947578-16-6

Ink Smith Publishing
710 S. Myrtle Ave Suite 209
Monrovia, CA, 91016

For my family

Who has now chosen to sleep with one eye open.

And to my cat

for always deciding to sit on top of my keyboard instead of her perfectly

comfortable bed.

Prologue

The loud drumming of my heart drowned out all thoughts. Somewhere in that mix of dull emotion was my conscience, and it continued to echo through my head in warning. Before it could coax me out of a rampage though, it faded to white noise. I was now alone with dark ambitions. I had come far enough now, and nothing would stop me.

I balanced the knife in my hand. Although the blade was not particularly short, it still felt too small. When I was young, I had pretended to be a knight preparing for battle. I would toss around a worn paper towel roll as if it were a sword. How I wished I had a steel blade of such proportions now. Revisiting my sweet past cemented the realization regarding my grim future. Now that I actually had a weapon, I hoped for something more dramatic. The kitchen knife I had brought from home would leave its mark, but it was still too light for my taste. The mild weight was almost unnoticeable in my grasp. My disappointment, however, was temporary. As I recalled my mission, my mood instantly lifted.

I crept down the hallway carefully, slithering across the shaggy white carpet as I approached the room where he was. If used correctly, even this knife would deal a fatal blow. I continued down the desolate span of walls toward the room that would change everything. Where he was resting and would take his final breaths. I would be the one to alter his fate as he had done to my father so many years ago. He was no innocent and that was the only reason I could think of to justify this bloodthirst.

My mind had always been a bit twisted, but I never allowed those crazed thoughts to surface. Until today. I always knew Cain was there, but had always managed to keep him at bay. When I was finally able to track down the filthy man who had killed my father, however, I made no attempt to hide Cain for the need for vengeance. The only thing that could stop this eternal, hollow ache would be to see his blood as it flowed from his unmoving body. Hopefully then, Cain would become more controllable.

I exhaled slowly and allowed the shaky breath to calm my nerves. As much as I had planned for this moment, I was still a bit unsure of how to feel. My stomach fluttered and I wondered if it was from fear or excitement. Probably the latter. I had been through every single scenario in my head to assure that I was prepared. So far everything had gone well. I had broken in easily without being noticed and was so close to the final phase of my revenge.

At last, I reached my destination. Using my free hand, I twisted the small doorknob and with a screech, the rusted hinges opened the door. I raised my knife menacingly and opened my mouth to speak. Unfortunately, my actions held no audience. To my distaste, I found the messy cave of a room abandoned. He was not here! *What the hell?* I had already scoured the house moments before and was sure that he would be here. I had checked to make sure his car was still there–for I had staked it out hours earlier. But with him not present, I realized my miscalculation. I had paid too much attention by making sure he couldn't escape through his car that I had forgotten to monitor the door. I dragged my hand down my face, mad at my own carelessness.

I wanted to scream in frustration, but forced myself to remain calm. The apartment complex–no matter how rundown–had other tenants. If I made any of them suspicious, my whole plan would fail. I could not risk letting this scheme fall apart. I only had one chance at revenge so I had to be careful.

With a plop, I plunked down on the small twin mattress. I needed a moment to think, but everything in the room was too distracting. The sheets on the bed were tangled and the cut-outs hanging on the grey walls were askew. It took every ounce of my strength not to fix everything around me. When it came to control I was obsessive. If something was not in perfect order, it was useless in my eyes. Control was everything, but we had a love/hate relationship. Although I hated that it forced me to contain Cain, it was the only thing that kept me in order. Control was the only thing that kept me sane. This normalcy I had acquired allowed me to pretend I was normal, even though it went so far against my nature. The dirty state of the room bothered me on a psychological level, but I couldn't expect too much from the lying scumbag that made it his home. Luckily, the thrill of the hunt was enough to take my mind off it.

I would wait for his return and then the kill would be mine. My first. He was nothing more than a pest to society and I would gladly get rid of the piece of trash. As much as I loved my father, his murder had been gratifying. I hadn't been the one to kill him, but his death made this moment possible. I did miss the distant, overbearing figure quite a bit, but his death had given me a reward. There was now a chance for me to relinquish control and release Cain in the name of revenge. That was the reasoning I had used to bypass my already slim conscience.

I had become lost in thought when the sound of a voice

brought me back to reality. I jumped out of the bed and grabbed my knife from the side table where I had placed it. With renewed my grip on the weapon, I crept out of the room, and into the narrow hallway. Staying glued to the wall, I glided past the unkempt laundry and bathrooms until I was inches from the living area. The living area contained the entrance to the apartment and the outdated kitchen where I assumed he now was.

I angled my blade, ready to emerge from my hiding space, when something stopped me in my tracks. Laughter. Only, it wasn't just his gruff laugh that echoed through the home. Joining the melody of amusement was a softer, shrill laugh. I retracted my forearm, held the knife, and stood very still. He wasn't alone.

I remained still until the noise settled. My breath rattled in my chest as I weighed my options. I couldn't make a move yet. As much as I would relish in a double kill, I couldn't afford that yet. I wasn't ready. I opted to wait until the second person left. To my delight, it was only seconds later that I heard the door shut with an exit. Without hesitation, I stormed into the crowded kitchen.

"What the hell?!" A raspy voice demanded as I burst around the corner.

The elderly man's features fell as I fully came into view—weapon and all. His thin, white lips parted as if he wanted to scream but was unable to. He was frozen. I used this to my advantage and didn't waste any time running over to where he was. I came up behind him, too quick for his old reflexes, stamped my hand over his mouth, and with my knife raised it to his throat.

The tip of my blade dragged along the loose skin of his neck slowly. I could end it quickly if I wanted to, but decided against it. This would be my first *real* kill. I wanted to savor it. This may be the only time I let Cain loose and I needed to make it good if I hoped to stop the never-ending hunger. Everything will have to return to normal after this and I will never have the chance to look back. For once in my life, I was letting Cain overcome my tainted mind and I wanted to enjoy it.

I pushed the heavy, old man against the counter and turned around to face him. His dull eyes were glazed from age, but I could still read their grey depths. He was afraid. Very afraid–no, terrified but also confused. He didn't know who I was. I had hoped he would recognize the icy blue eyes and sharp features that connected me to my deceased father but he seemed to be drawing a blank. Since I was going to prolong the inevitable, I decided to grant him some answers.

"It's Sylas," I declared as I twirled the blade around in my dominant hand.

He shook his head solemnly and I sighed. I was expecting

too much out of the dirty geezer. "Sylas Hamel," I restated more firmly. I knew my last name hit its mark when his eyes widened. "Ah, now you get it, huh?" I repositioned my knife against his neck, but retracted my hand from his mouth. If he wanted to talk, I was willing to listen. Nothing would change my mind, of course, but groveling was always amusing.

"Is this is about your father?" he stuttered. Sweat dripped down his bald head and he raised a greasy finger to wipe at it. Disgusting.

"It may be," I confirmed.

"It was a long time ago. See, I never realized he had a son. Please, you've gotta believe me–I never meant to hurt nobody!" He groveled. He was visibly shaking in his oversized polo and stained khakis. Gross.

I shook my head to indicate he had given me the wrong answer, "You truly are no better than swine. At least pigs are smart," I let out a hysterical laugh. "Even if I was here on behalf of my father, do you think that pathetic apology would work?"

"You—you're not?"

"Here for my father?" Another laugh, slightly lower than the first, escaped my mouth. I was no longer the one in control. Cain claimed me and I was merely an observer, "No. This is for *me*."

In one swift motion, the knife sliced through the old man's scaly skin. I put more force behind it than I had intended, but it hit its mark perfectly nonetheless.

I stepped back, knife in tow, as he collapsed with a gasping breath. I could see from the desperation in his eyes that he wanted to scream, but all I could hear was a muffled gurgle as blood spilled down his fat chin. A crimson geyser exploded from his damaged neck and splattered in a morbid pattern across the floor. The white tiles grew red in color as the scarlet liquid burst out of the severed veins. My victim splashed around in his own ruby puddle a moment before growing eerily still.

I was barely aware of the sound from behind as an exhilarating rush of adrenaline flooded my system. I wanted to scream in pleasure. *This is the ultimate control. I have the power to decide it all.* I roared in laughter as Cain continued to direct my mind. He wanted to revel in his own creation, but was stopped short.

A gasp from behind forced me to turn around. I met the gaze of a strange woman who stood in the doorway. I was instantly reverted to my normal, non-demonic self. Her look of blank horror told me all I needed to know. She saw it all. There was a witness to Cain, my inner evil, and I, for the first time ever, had no idea what to do.

Chapter 1

I stood there, crouched over my dead victim, as I maintained eye contact with the complication. Her soft, blue eyes widened in fear. I stretched back to reveal my full height as I strode over to where she remained frozen. The knife, still dripped with blood, never left my grasp as I stalked toward my next victim. I had not planned on taking two lives, but what else could I do? I was a selfish and lethal being only concerned with myself. I did regret that she would fall prey to Cain, though. My moral compass might have been skewed, but I could still detect good from evil. She was definitely on the purer side of life.

Her petite frame racked with shivers from my closed proximity and I stalled for a moment. I observed the way her deep brown hair engulfed her narrow face and the trembling of her lip. She was a far cry from the vulgar being I had just killed, and I grew hesitant. *Should I slay her as I had done with the stilled body at my feet?* I shook my head to clear my thoughts and proceeded. It felt wrong now, but once Cain was in control, my limited sympathy would vanish.

She took a small step backwards, only to be stopped by the wall. She palmed at the barricade desperately while still facing me. Her hands reached out from behind her in hopes of finding an exit, but the wall was devoid of any doors. She was trapped and began to panic. I frowned at her mortification. Normally, I would relish in another's fright, but now my stomach settled uncomfortably. A disturbed thought slammed through my mind. *Am I really that menacing?* Aside from the scarlet liquid that coated my arms as evidence of my crime, I did not find myself too scary. Intimidating, yes, but not from my monstrous actions. I am an intelligent, young businessman–my intimidation tactics are what have taken me so far–but never had I expected my calculating nature to be received with fear. Even the man I had just slaughtered didn't look twice until he saw my weapon. I let out a deep sigh. This mental conflict is exasperating.

I raised my knife up lazily. A shimmer across the stained weapon forced me to hesitate. A tiny, distorted reflection of me was just barely visible along the length of the blade. I did a double take at the partially imagined picture before I looked back at her.

So, this is what she sees.

I had forgotten my unusual state of dress might affect her impression. I was normally clean, crisp, and well-dressed in preparation for my office career. Today, however, I had a much more disheveled look. In case things had gone awry, I was prepared to make a fast escape and be sure that I couldn't be recognized. I had succeeded in my disguise. Even I could barely discern who I was underneath the unkempt facade. I donned a worn, grey shirt which had sleeves that grew tight around my biceps and dark blue jeans. My messy hair and faint stubble only added to the rugged effect. My short, blonde hair fell in loose tangles around my head. The soft platinum locks curled around my ears and stopped just short of my collar. I swatted at the strands that stopped just short of my eyes. I was growing irritated and out of control.

Clearing my throat, I moved until only inches separated me and my statuesque maiden. She dropped her head at our closeness and I noted her fists clenched tightly at her sides. She would be deprived of movement if it weren't for the shaky rise and fall of her torso. My chest ached sorely at the thought of taking that breath away. There is something so delicate about her that I had trouble wanting to kill her.

Where is Cain, my persistent bloodlust, when I need him most? Is Cain abandoning me when I actually require his presence?

I had to remind myself of the consequences of not acting on Cain's wishes. My world revolved around me. I never denied the existence of other celestial bodies in the universe, but nothing else has had nearly enough gravitational force to knock me out of my selfish orbit. Until today.

Towered over the shrinking figure of my temporary sun, I stared deeply. I placed my forefinger under her chin and lifted her head. The slight movement was enough to reconnect our gazes. Her bright, blue eyes shone dully. Water began to brim in the crevice of her eyelids. Displeased by the way the moisture obscured her beautiful irises, and I was overcome with an urge to swipe away the forming tears. Nearly lost in the moment, I refocused at the task at hand. As I detached my finger from her jaw, my bloodied digit left behind a red smear. The stain was enough to bring me back to my grim reality.

The whispers of death had surrounded me my whole life, but today was the first time I was weak enough to succumb. In one moment, I had changed the course of my destiny. As soon as I submitted to those unholy urges, I became one with Cain. No longer was I plagued by death, but I had become the face of death. I was officially a killer and would never be able to stop again. The pale young women in front of me may have had, at one time, been able to save me. Now it was too late. My one chance at salvation had evaporated with one tactful slice. The race against Cain had been lost. She was so close to me, but yet so far away. My reaction to her showed that there was something else that rivaled Cain. Unfortunately, Cain had been kept at bay for so long. I was not toying with evil. I was that evil.

I closed my eyes, reopened them, and watched her lucid expression. I felt a wave of sorrow. She had stood there motionless the entire time–her fight or flight response severely neglected. She was a small rabbit, all untainted and pure. It felt wrong, but I had no choice. I didn't like preying on the weak, but it was a matter of self-preservation. I could not risk her finding out my identity and tattling on me to the police.

It was time to finish the innocent lamb before me. I took one last look into her pretty face before swinging my blade. Before the knife could slice her delicate skin, a soft voice sounded.

"Sorry," she whispered as she ducked out of the way.

Sorry? My confusion was all the distraction she needed. She ran under my arm and slammed headfirst into my chest. Taken off guard, I dropped the knife with a grunt. She didn't wait to wallow in her victory and quickly darted around me before I could grab hold of her. She was too fast and I cursed myself as I stumbled over my own feet. The little minx was making a show out of this! I growled and made chase while she dashed into the kitchen. She slipped behind the counter, leaving a wide berth between her and the lifeless body. Opening a drawer from beneath the grey, colorless countertops, she withdrew something silver. I froze and watched her. If she managed to get ahold of a weapon, I risked trouble. I misjudged her. From first glance, I presumed she was innocent. Of course, no one so simple would think to fight back and not turn a weapon on me.

Just as I was about to rethink my earlier reaction, she surprised me.

Huddled at the edge of the kitchen, she stood and extended a fork. I nearly laughed at the absurdity. Her defense mechanism consisted entirely of a piece of silverware. If the forming bruise against my sternum hadn't reminded me of the situation, I would have doubled over in a state of crazed humor.

"A fork? Really?" I scoffed as I narrowed our distance. She slashed the fork through the air in the hope that it would repel my presence. Unfortunately for her, it had the opposite effect. Within an instant, I was upon her, and she was cornered. "If I was a salad, I would be terrified but since I'm no meager mix of vegetables, that little trident isn't going to cut it."

She pressed the metallic object against me and I could feel the prongs pricking my shoulder. It was nothing more than a tickle. She was holding back. Aimed correctly, the fork could leave a nasty mark but I knew she didn't have the physique for such an action. As it was, her threatening actions were already taking a toll on her fragile mentality. She was shaking badly and her eyes were beginning to water. My wry grin faded. She was scared and it bothered me. It was as if I was physically affected by her emotional upset.

Crap! Sylas, come on! Finish it!

Whatever she was doing to me, it was unproductive. I was intrigued by the unique reactions to her, but I didn't have the time to digest it thoroughly. I was a born killer whose instincts only faded on the rarest occasions–this being one of them. My suffocating need for blood was dialed back to a tolerable level and I was able to focus on what was in front of me. I should have been excited by this revelation–I certainly was intrigued–but she was more than just an ordinary person. She was the only one right now who could bring me down; a witness to my crime. She had been the one to see my lapse in control and there was no way she could stay alive after doing so. No matter what this connection was, self- preservation would always prevail.

I grabbed her arm and pried the fork from her grasp, "Not today, dear cabbage." I spoke softly while I placed the fork behind me on the counter. I was surprised by the sincere humor in my voice. I was trying to calm her down, but I wasn't sure why. She would be dead soon anyway. What did I care if she felt comfortable? I didn't need her to cozy up to me.

Apparently, my humor wasn't relaxing. She let out a sob and dropped her head. Her shoulders shrugged up and down as her cries rang out. She looked around desperately, but when I grabbed her wrists; she understood there was no escape. This realization only caused her sobs to increase in intensity.

This was my chance. She was giving up, and it would be a swift kill. I sighed and readied myself to accept her surrender, but something pricked my mind. "Earlier," I spoke, "You said 'sorry'. Why?"

She ignored my question and lowered herself. I released her wrists, and allowed her to sink to the ground. Her thin, white blouse and tight jeans wrinkled as she curled her arms around her knees.

Her mortification made something tingle in the back of my skull. It was inconceivable, but her weak resolve left me strangely unsettled. Regardless of my untimely sympathy, I was not finished. I wanted an answer. I squatted down until we were level, "Before you hit my chest and tried to get away from me, you apologized. I don't understand why you did that since you are the victim in this scenario," I motioned to where the old man's corpse was growing cold.

She closed her eyes and let out a whistled breath. Her face was wet from crying and her thin layer of makeup was smudged. "I don't know," she admitted. Apparently realizing she was not getting out alive until she spoke, she decided to keep talking.

It was peculiar how much emphasis was placed on those last words. It was as if some final plea would cause the executioner to grant mercy. Either that or a condemned victim merely wished to maximize their final breath. Personally, I preferred silence and saw no value in begging. If anything, futile chatter incensed me further. With the pitiful shell of a woman in my presence, however, I didn't sense the least bit of irritation. Alternatively, I wanted to continue our conversation. Clinging to her words, I watched each shallow breath transform into a vocalized thought.

"I just don't know how anything like this can happen," her volume increased enough at the end that I no longer had to lean in to catch every word. She grappled at her necklace with her right hand. Grasping the small golden cross that hung at the end of the chain, she exhaled slowly.

Her religion and behavior made it very clear just how different we were. She was far more righteous than I, and I could only guess what it was that made her so interesting. I had the strangest urge to protect her from my own crimes. She was not a victim for my taste but was on a separate level. She was…pure.

Something about that purity made her appear weak. As crazy as it was, a beast like me could not stand to hunt innocent prey. I was a lion who killed hyenas, but protected rabbits. No amount of carnage or evil would make me flinch, but bring a small rabbit into the equation and I went berserk. What was so odd though was that there had only ever been two rabbits in my life. My mother and little sister were the only people I had no desire to and would not kill. They, however, did not invoke such a strong need to protect. The shaken, crying mess before me was another species entirely.

These were not ordinary circumstances, though, and there was no saving this creature. "I'm afraid it's my turn to apologize now," I said with a hint of remorse.

I moved my hands from her cheeks and down to her neck. I tensed my fingers as they wrapped around her slender throat. Strangulation was not my preferred method, but I didn't have the time to grab my knife. I feared if I prolonged this any further I wouldn't be able to go through with it. Even though I so often fantasized about releasing Cain and killing others, I found that I wished for nothing more than to let this pretty little complication go.

The one time I needed Cain, he disappeared.

I forced my fingers to tighten against my will. The more my hands clenched, the easier it was to feel her arteries. Something about the way her veins throbbed against my touch made me recoil. With a gasp, I relinquished my grip. My arms fell to my sides. I was defeated both physically and mentally. Never had the thought of death bothered me to the point of physical disgust but, when I was an iron grip away from killing her, I couldn't help but feel sick.

Her hands flew to her throat as she gasped for air desperately. She coughed raggedly and I felt bad for causing her pain. Yes, I, the mad killer, felt *bad*.

"Come on," I ordered as I stood up. I grabbed her arm and pulled her along with me. Her blue eyes swirled in confusion and I added, "You're getting out of here."

Still in disbelief, she froze under my power. I ground my teeth together before mustering a smile. It was my signature grin. It had served me well in business, but it was not charisma I was going for this time. I was trying my best to reassure her through nonverbal cues.

"Really?" she uttered in question. Her voice cracked and I imagined it was still raw from my touch. Her throat was smeared with blood, but underneath I knew there were marks from my manhandling.

I rubbed my temples angrily. My head throbbed. I had no idea how to handle this, "Yes! Now hurry before I change my mind!" I roared. It was a stupid idea. Although I acknowledged the idiocy, I couldn't kill her.

She nodded obediently and began to turn away. I stopped her when I

noticed the phone poking out of her back pocket. I reached for it and snatched it out of her jeans. She jumped at my touch.

"Wha—"

"Now, go!"

Without looking back, she ran as fast as her legs would carry her. She flung the door open and escaped.

I eyed the phone in hand before stuffing it into my pocket. I had grabbed it just in case. Something told me, I would need to find her again in case her witness status was needed. I also hated the thought of letting such a strange woman get away. No one had ever managed to complete subdue Cain's need for blood. I wanted to know why. I let her escape and I needed to know how I was capable of such an unorganized action.

I walked over to the sink and cleansed my bloodied hands. I needed to hurry and get out of here. For all I knew, she was calling the police right now. I may have taken her phone, but it wouldn't be too hard to find someone with a device capable of dialing nine-one-one.

I turned off the faucet and made my way to the small half bathroom. I had to ignore the mess of toothpaste and hair along the counter and did a once over in the mirror. I looked clean enough not to raise any suspicions. I looked a bit gruff, but not to the point that it screamed criminal. In fact, my rugged appearance might have been considered fashionable. While I didn't see the attractiveness in my frazzled golden hair and worn denim jeans, I would use it to my advantage. A pretty face went a long way in this twisted world, and I appreciated my chiseled features and haunting blue eyes, for they granted me many perks. A built-in camouflage system is how I referred to it. I, even in my most crazed states, could hide in plain sight. No one ever looked twice at me because of Cain. Appearance is such an important part of first impressions, and I was glad of my Adonis qualities.

With a huff, I exited the bathroom. I grabbed my knife, wiped it down with a small cloth I found, and tucked it back with the other knifes in the kitchen. I contemplated cleaning the fork she had used against me to erase any prints, but instead opted to keep it for myself. A memento of sorts.

I left the clammy apartment as quickly and stealthily as possible. The whole building was rundown and I was happy about the lack of security cameras. Still, I didn't want any unneeded attention. I slithered down the musky hallway and took the stairs out of the complex.

As soon as I stepped outside, I was greeted by the bustling sounds of the city. A cool, autumn breeze whipped my hair around and goosebumps rose on my exposed forearms. With a shrug, I hurried along the sidewalk. Traffic was not too bad for a Friday afternoon and I settled into a rhythm with the other people walking along the downtown area. I easily managed to blend into one of the groups marching along and I followed suit until I arrived at the sketchy garage where I had parked my car.

As I stepped into the silver BMW, a sense of calm I had melted away as the scenes from the apartment replayed in my head. It wasn't the fact that I was officially a murderer that bothered me; it was the thought that I could be caught. If I was discovered, the façade I had spent my whole life fabricating would crumble. I couldn't stand the idea of everything I worked for, would vanish because of one slip of inhumanity. I was confident I could get away with killing him, but having a witness threw a major wrench in those plans.

I needed to do something. I was going stir-crazy sitting in the front seat of my car. I needed to talk without really talking. Get my emotions out without stating their cause. As much as I didn't want to risk spilling my guts; there was only one person I could turn to. Reaching into my pocket, I pulled out everything. A wallet, two phones, keys, and a fork were sprawled across the leather interior of the shotgun seat. I plucked my phone out of the pile and reluctantly dialed my speed dial number one on the apple device.

Three rings went by before an answer, "Hello?" "I screwed up."

"Sylas?" she started, "What happened?" I identified worry amidst her flat tone.

I had never once in our time together told her of the things that plagued me but she always felt the need to ask. "It's not important, Stell," I answered defiantly. This was our usual MO— never actually say what the issues are, but continue to converse anyway. It was just how we worked.

She sighed. Even for someone as unenthusiastic as Stella, she sounded tired, "Fine. So, what do you want? I'm busy, Sy, and I've got a lot going on right now."

I didn't even bother to ask what she was busy with. We were close siblings, but we never actually indulged in each other's lives. Neither of us could stand to say what affected us, though I knew her actions could never compare to mine. I could imagine my little sister on the other side of the phone, rolling her eyes at our unproductive conversation. Although a bit pessimistic and aloof, she had a big heart. She, like me, was never one to share what was on her mind and had trouble developing bonds with others. She only had a few friends and was lonely–although she would never admit it. That's why she, despite the annoying lack of details in them, loved my calls. "Just needed your voice to refocus," I admitted. It was partially true. I felt the sudden longing for companionship, but I was also scared about the authorities finding the body and linking me to the crime. I needed someone to calm my nervous jitters, and Stella was the only one available.

Another sigh. "Okay, bro. Tell me what you want to hear," A pitch of amusement littered her voice. She didn't know what had me so ruffled, but I'm sure she enjoyed hearing that her perfect big brother screwed up.

Twisted humor ran in the family, I guess. What wasn't shared in our DNA, though, was the need to kill and I would take that secret with me to the grave. I finally responded, "Oh, just be sure to mention—"

A laugh ignited on the other side. She was enjoying my need for camaraderie.

I paused before starting again. To humor myself I said, "I could use a reminder of how successful and rich I am."

Stella grew quiet. I grinned at her silence. It was a bit of a low blow, but fine in the name of comedy. "For someone so successful you seem to need all the moral support I give," She let out a snort at her own joke.

"Very funny," I spoke. The truth of the matter, though, was that I needed her reinforcement. She was the only person I whole heartedly conversed with; even if half of what I said were lies.

"Alright, Sy–I gotta go. Seriously, though, I'm sure everything's fine. You're a good guy who wouldn't hurt a fly!"

Oh, the irony!

"Yeah, okay," was all I could muster. "Bye," A click on the other end told me Stella had hung up.

I rolled my head along my shoulders in an attempt to ease some of the tension. My muscles felt like they were on fire. I dropped my phone back onto the seat. I buckled myself in, and turned the keys in the ignition. The car roared to life and I felt the rhythmic hum of the engine underneath me. Before I drove off, though, I was overcome by the urge to look through the phone I had stolen. I needed to learn everything I could about the owner and the anticipation was killing me. It was about an hour drive back to my estate, and I was too impatient to wait that long.

To my surprise—and delight—there was no password on the lock screen and I gained instant access. It was like opening a door that allowed me to glimpse into the life of my newest obsession.

I wasn't aware how long I sat there, car idling, as I scrolled through the smart phone in search of answers. I paused when I found the information I had been looking for. I discovered her name along with a gaggle of other personal data.

Piper Rowan. Female. Twenty-six years old. And soon to be either my second kill or my first treasure to lock away.

Chapter 2

He was all I could see. His blue eyes tinted with an innocently icy hue were suffocated by madness. His beautiful face was twisted by an unrelenting force.

I had just witnessed a horrible crime. Evil had haunted his regal features and soaked into his every pore. But the effects of the darkness were gone as soon as I spoke. Like being flashed out of a frenzy, the murderous man regained some elements of humanity. I had not believed my eyes at the time and, had it not been for the angry marks around my neck, I would have thought I imagined it. What had been my way of helping out my elderly neighbor ended in murder.

I shook my head violently in an attempt to erase the horrific scene. It had been several days since the incident and I was still plagued by that murderous man. I hadn't even bothered to return to my apartment afterward. The moment he allowed for my escape, I ran. My life depended on getting as far away as possible. Luckily, I had managed to snag the spare bedroom at an old friend's house. We had been roommates the first few years of college and because I had always looked past some of her scandalous moments, we had developed a 'don't ask/don't tell' policy. One call from some hotel's landline later and my shelter was accounted for. I could tell that Arial was curious, but I refrained from answering any questions. My call had come out of the blue and she was so surprised that I needed her help that it was only natural she was suspicious. Still, being the gracious host she was, I was given free board. It would have been a lot more fun to catch up with an old acquaintance had the circumstances been different.

I busied myself cleaning the small room I had been granted. I had to keep myself occupied otherwise I would go stir-crazy. Too preoccupied folding the cotton blanket on the bed, I didn't hear Arial approach.

"You could use some sun," a nasally voice scolded.

I spun around to find my friend propped up against the doorframe. She filled up the entrance with her tall, gangly frame. I forced a smile, "Pardon?"

She waved her slender hand in dismissal. "Don't play coy, Piper. You may refuse to give me all the details, but something is definitely up."

I shook my head slowly. "It's nothing," I assured her.

Apparently, my trifling words were not convincing enough and Arial rolled her eyes in response. "You–little miss preppy–would never show up on my doorstep, without her cellphone, randomly. I'm not going to pry for all the details, but you seem shaken. You've done nothing but hide in this room for the past two days and something needs to change. Go outside and get some fresh air because whatever it is, you are going to have to face it sooner or later."

My heart squeezed at the devout loyalty of my friend. She was trying to help me even though I refused to tell her what was wrong. There were few people that I could have contacted under such extreme circumstances, but she had let me in without a second thought. Of course, I wanted to tell her what happened, but there was no way to bring up a murder nonchalantly. I had already used her smart phone to leave an anonymous tip to the police, but other than that I didn't want to involve her in any way.

"I'm fine, really."

Arial sighed in defeat, flicked a perfectly styled curl over her shoulder, and eyed me suspiciously, "Are you sure there's not anything I can do?"

I was about to deny her attempt to help, when an idea struck.

"Actually," I began as I spotted the phone sticking out of her unnecessarily short shorts, "I didn't have my phone because it was missing. Do you still have the 'Find My iPhone' app on your phone and is it still connected?" After losing her phone in a series of drunken escapades years ago, I had forced Arial to do the sharing plan with me so I could locate it. I always had to be the responsible one, but I hoped this time she would be able to help. To my relief, she still had the app.

Arial's dark eyes flickered in excitement, "Of course!" she said as she clapped her hands together in delight. Her mahogany skin absorbed the minimal lighting of the room in a way that drew all attention to her. She had a cool confidence about her and, to my jealousy, succeeded in all social situations. Academically, it was another story. She was not necessarily dumb, but she had never shown any motivation toward her studies.

For someone who I had always considered lazy and unfocused during our school years, she certainly got excited over the idea of tracking down my phone. To her it was an adventure, but for me it was a way to find justice. Although I hadn't seen any news reports about the incident at my apartment, I had a horrible feeling that the killer would escape unpunished. He had managed to nab my phone before I ran for my life. If I could track it down, there was a chance that I could find whoever was responsible for the crime. I had not considered it before, but Arial's reminder of my absent phone helped all the pieces click together in my head.

"Great!" I responded with false excitement.

Arial handed me her phone that had been covered in a sparkly pink case. I grimaced at the overly feminine touch. I was a person that never appreciated personalization. Efficiency over appearance had been drilled into my head over the years to minimize distractions. The only accessory I had ever used on myself was the golden cross that hung around my neck. It had been a gift from my mother and it had disgusted me how the criminal looked at it. That sinner had dared to smirk at the sight of my religion. *Well, the joke is on him now.* If I found where my phone was, it would be I who looked at him with disdain as his wrongfully attractive face was behind bars–where he belonged.

I entered my phone's information into the app and handed it back to Arial. Although I had grown somewhat accustomed to the latest technology, I was far from an expert. Aside from emails, calls, and the occasional game; I was unfamiliar with modern devices.

I waited in anticipation, my stomach in tight knots while awaiting the information to appear. I was scared at what I might find. What if I found the location but it was wrong and aggravated the killer further. Before I went further down into over analyze mode, Arial's shrill laugh interrupted my thoughts.

"What?" I asked in confusion. Laughter was not the reaction I expected. "Oh geez, Piper," Arial said in between bouts of giggles, "And here I thought you left it in a bar or something. I was expecting you to be in real trouble, girl. Of course, it was nothing," she snorted.

"How do you know it was nothing?" I retorted defensively. Had she known what had occurred she wouldn't have dared to so easily dismiss it.

She handed the phone to me with a knowing look. I snatched it from her outstretched hand and nearly gasped at the location on the screen. The address indicated was my own. I took a small step back, mortified by the result. He let me go, but the last thing I expected was for my phone to be returned. Maybe he had changed his mind about my fate and this was merely a trap to lure me in. I frowned at the thought.

"Need a ride?" Arial offered, "I know you wanted to stay here a little longer but we should probably go grab that phone."

"No!" I shouted more forcefully than intended. At Arial's furrowed brow, I added, "I'll just leave it there. it's not that important," I couldn't think of a better excuse. I would eventually need my phone, but I couldn't risk going back there.

"Are you kidding me?" She laughed, "I couldn't last five minutes without my cell! It'll be quick—can't have you always using mine for however long you plan to stay." She drifted off at the end of her sentence and raised a brow.

I understood the gesture. "I won't stay much longer," I promised. Arial was a good friend, although not always the most responsible. She was happy to offer me shelter, but her generosity had its limit. She had also been pushing me to face whatever it was that had led me astray in the first place. The more I avoided the topic of being away from home the more suspicious she grew, but I couldn't return to my small apartment. If my phone was there then he was probably there too. I shuddered slightly. If that killer was there then I could alert the police. I could tell that he was the slippery type, one who could probably evade the police forever, unless I did something. "On second thought," I proclaimed, "I really should get it."

"Alright, let's go," Arial answered. She walked over to the kitchen counter and grabbed the keys to her Jeep. Twirled them around her index finger, and lifted her chin. The black curls encircled her head and bobbed up at the motion.

"What?"

"You look a little spooked."

"I'm not spooked—just deep in thought," I defended.

She laughed and headed to the door. Before we left, I grabbed a light blue parka I found draped across the couch and shrugged it on. With winter fast approaching, the air held an unmistakable chill and I was not a fan of the cold. Arial, of course, did not bother to cover up her revealing denim shorts or cropped top. I decided against scolding her on her lack of warm clothing. Too many times in the past had I suggested she cover up the unnecessary amount of skin only to be referred to as a prude. I, of course, only tried to protect her from the unruly stares of those men who could only gawk at her appearance. Arial was beautiful with her ideal proportions, but there was such a thing as overdoing it. I always opted for a more natural, conservative look. It was the way I had been raised and a habit I knew I could never shake.

Once we reached the newly modeled red Jeep that Arial prided herself on, I clambered into the front seat. I was appalled by the roofless version she had gone for at this time of year. I made a show of shivering and reaching for the seat warmer when she asked if anything was wrong.

"It's November for Christ's sake! How can you not bother to put together the rest of your car?"

18

"It's November," She responded, "Which means it's not yet winter. I personally enjoy a bit of wind on my face," she added as the pair of stylish round sunglasses that had been rested on her head were flicked into place.

After my final grumbling about how summer ended months ago, the car ride continued with bland commentary consisting of idle chitchat. Arial went on about the relationships between several people whose names I had heard so many times before, but never listened enough to care what was currently infringing upon their lives. The way she always mentioned them made it clear that they were an important part of her social life. Even though these people had no contribution in my life, I would often zone out and let my friend do all the talking. For Arial's sake, I indulged in the classic set of nods and vague answers to allow her to finish the conversation. I laughed at the appropriate spots, always knew the slight wrinkles forming around her mouth indicated a necessary humorous response. After years of college, I easily learned how to hold a one-sided conversation with the gossip heavy Arial. While my one word responses were enough to make it appear I was attentive to what Arial was saying, my mind was elsewhere.

Striking blonde hair flocked around a sharp featured face in a state of disarray. It would have fooled anyone in assuming it was normally that messy, but I was convinced otherwise. Every stain on the shirt and tangle in his hair was chaotic, but methodical. Asymmetry in an organized manner. His messy appearance was nothing more than a disguise. The blood that stained his hands and the rags he donned would have made him appear of the lower class, but there was something in his eyes. Our encounter had been brief, but within those icy marine irises there was more than just simple hatred. There was an unmistakable intelligence that radiated from him. He was not the average criminal. The way he stood without the slightest hint of a slouch told me much about him. He was someone used to power. What had happened was not the usual crime of passion, but something far more sinister. For what I saw deep inside him on that faithful day was not the satisfaction of someone whose plans of revenge had come to fruition. No, what I witnessed was a predator hunting down his prey and reveling in the power he gained as he destroyed life. He didn't kill for hunger or necessity like a predator in the wild, but for sport. The look of exhilaration he had as the blood spewed from his victim before he noticed my presence haunted my nightmares even now. Had he been a lion; he would have purred as his bloodlust was fulfilled.

The car came to a halt and I shook myself once before I looked up at my building. The large, grey structure seemed to loom ominously as I forced myself to exit the car. One quick wave to Arial, the small Jeep sputtered forward and left. I was alone on the street. Despite it being midday I felt as if I was shrouded by shadows. Arial had made plans to go shopping at a mall nearby and although she would come pick me up at a later time, I was on my own until she returned.

I wasn't stupid. There was no way I was going to just storm in and risk seeing him again. Instead, I would call the police and make sure that they cleared everything first. If he was there and they managed to capture him, many lives would be spared no doubt.

With my head held high, I marched into the front lobby. The whole place was shabby, crumbling, and grimy; but I had called it my home for almost a year. It was all I could afford at the time and if I had ever needed a better reason to move out, surely this was it. I had never liked the place much with all its bugs and lack of security, but due to its location; I had been willing to ignore those minor details. Now, of course, I wish I hadn't.

I walked up to the reception desk, managed to get ahold of a phone, and called the police. During my nine-one-one call, I stated that I felt as if I had been threatened by someone and I believed them to be in my apartment. It was not a total lie, for I feared he might be there, but I failed to mention anything regarding the murder.

The petite young receptionist had been too engulfed in her magazine across the counter to overhear my phone call and when I returned the phone to her, she smiled obliviously. I shook my head aimlessly. It was better if I didn't cause a commotion now, but there would be drama later when the police arrived.

There were no sirens signaling the arrival of my help. Instead, the police car slid to a smooth stop in front of the building quietly. Two people hopped out of the car and I rushed to meet them as they entered through the front doors.

"Are you the one who called this in?" The first of the two figures asked with a casual wave that came with experience.

I nodded curtly, "Yes sir."

The burly man raked a broad hand through his noticeable greying hair. "Alright then," he started, "Let's go." Boredom dripped from his professional tone.

The second officer, who was shorter and leaner than the first, glanced around the complex without much interest. The duo followed as I led them to the stairs. There was no rush in their steps as they settled into a slow stride. It was as if they were here merely out of obligation. They must have thought this was a boring and pointless case.

I squirmed slightly at their quick dismissal. To them, I was probably just another paranoid woman. I was irritated by the notion they found no importance in my claim! If I was correct, a killer would be brought to justice!

Once on in the stairwell, the smaller man asked, "Which floor?"

"Fourth."

He raised an eyebrow and the other officer whistled. "What?"

The older male cleared his throat when his colleague remained silent, "Was just wondering if you were going to say fifth floor, that's all."

"Why?" I questioned with feigned innocence, even though I knew the answer. The fifth floor was where the murder had taken place. I had been on the fifth floor, helping the elderly man unpack his groceries when it had all occurred. "Well, I'm sure you are aware by now of what happened there…between the cops and the news," He spoke as we reached the final steps leading to my floor. With one big push, the heavy door was opened, and showed the long row of doors.

"Third one on the left," I announced as I handed one of them my key. The older of the two accepted it. He motioned for me to stay behind as he withdrew his gun. His partner quickly followed suit, "We'll make sure nobody is here."

It was all part of a routine and I'm sure they doubted that anyone dangerous really lurked in my small home, but I found comfort in their precaution.

After what felt like an eternity, they reemerged. "All clear," they repeated in unison.

"Are you sure?" I stuttered hysterically. I wasn't convinced it was safe. The scrawny one walked up to me and placed a hand on my shoulder,

"Everything's fine ma'am, nothing to worry about."

"Just a false alarm," the first officer responded disappointedly.

They left as quickly and silently as they came and I found myself all alone in the hallway. It took all my might to walk toward the door and not run away. Just because no one was there didn't mean someone hadn't been, at one point. With a deep breath, I entered my miniscule apartment. I was immediately overcome with the feeling of chills being raked down my spine.

"It's wrong somehow," I mumbled aloud. I glanced around the main room quickly. I lived modestly and the only things of value, my computer and small TV, were un-tampered. With those in place, it would be hard to play the break-in card, but deep down I knew someone had been here.

As my eyes roamed the perimeter, I noticed something resting on the small sill of the window. It was my phone. I grabbed it hastily and unlocked it with the slide of my finger. The first screen that pulled up was all of my text messages. The one that was currently showing on the screen was addressed from and sent to me. The mysterious thing about it was that I had never messaged myself.

I repeated the words out loud as if somehow that would decrease their magnitude.

See you soon.

I grabbed any essential belongings and ran out the door.

Chapter 3

The alleyway was dark and unforgiving. Only the little white cloud that sputtered out with each breath reminded me that light ever existed. Dusk had settled and only the streetlights and stars continued to disfigure the night with their greedy rays.

It was an evening ripe with the scent of death. I bent over the brick maze and retrieved my knife from the throat of my latest victim. He was a common man stupid enough to use the privacy of an alley for a phone call. After I ended his life, I had made sure to turn off, and pocket his cell so it could not be tracked. His rapidly cooling skin glowed pale in the moonlight beside the puddle of red, I smiled, and closed my eyes to make sure the scene was committed to memory. I didn't plan on forgetting any of my victims.

"Number four," I spoke as I towered over the corpse. The shriveled shell of the person could not respond and I reveled in the silence. The silence that *I* had delivered. It had been four weeks since my first kill and the encounter with the future damsel I planned to capture. In the meantime, I had murdered three more times. The old man who killed my father, a woman who smoked alone at night, a drunken man from a bar, and the commoner at my feet made up my tally. Each time was the same; a quick attack with a knife that ended with a slashed throat. I would watch the life drain from each person before I would leave without the slightest trace.

I had no false pre-notions about what I was or what I was doing. I am evil and kill whenever, for the sole purpose of enjoyment. I was not, in any way, trying to better the world or serve some ridiculous cult. I sought blood because I wanted to. The temporary euphoria after each murder granted me solace from Cain's voice inside my head. He would return soon but for now, I was alone. My bloodlust was sated.

I exited the alley when I found the street was clear. I strolled out confidently with a bright smile. The security cameras in this part of town were shoddy at best and in the dark, I wouldn't be distinguished from any other male in a dark hoodie.

As I walked down the street, I placed my hands in the pocket of my sweatshirt and palmed the blade I had just used. It was sticky where the blood had stained it, but it could still be reused. I had a bit of a walk ahead since I decided to play it safe and parked farther away whenever the mood struck. I started storing baby wipes in my car. Blood was the sign of pain and, while it was philosophically gratifying at the time of my kills, it was a gross substance. It also had the tendency to stain.

I traveled down the empty street and began to laugh. Maniacally cackling, I must have appeared deranged, but it didn't matter. I had stayed away from the area where I worked, but it wouldn't have made a difference. My hair was shaggy and I wore a loose fitted hoodie and dark jeans. No one, even those closest to me, would have recognized me in this state. Normally, I was professional and controlling. This extended to my clothes as well: A tailored suit and slicked back hair were all those associated with me. They were all fools, but I guess I couldn't blame them. Humans were selfish with egocentric natures that made it impossible for them to imagine others differently, because it would require too much thought outside of their own personal worries.

The drive home was long and smooth. I had built my estate far from the inner city. While others might dread the long commute, I always found it relaxing. It was a necessary security measure that my house be located far from anyone else. I needed and loved my privacy.

As the gates pulled back, I eased down the long driveway. Halfway to the main house, I was greeted by a chorus of barking. I smiled at the sound of my pets' music. I could picture all four mutts wiggling in their positions, awaiting my arrival. While they made lots of noise, they were trained too well to leave the spots I had assigned them unless I said they could. I had gotten the dogs several years ago, in one of my spontaneous moments, but I have never regretted it. The dogs had been an added security measure, but I also greatly enjoyed their company.

Once inside the massive house, I changed my clothes and stashed away my weapon before calling to my canine guards.

"Simon, free. Daisy, free. Rebel, free. Buster, free," When I trained them, I made sure that they only followed commands if their name was attached, so they would only listen to those who knew them.

At the sound of my words, a barrage of paws scraped along the marble floors and echoed throughout the mansion. All four of the large breeds lumbered toward me and I kneeled down to pet them. Buster, the large russet-furred Chow mix, dropped to the floor and rolled over on his back. He chortled as I rubbed his soft tummy. Rebel was the next one to make his way over and whined for attention. I turned to the demanding Rottweiler and scratched him between his ears. After I finished rewarding those two with praise, I turned toward my more patient dogs. Simon, the white Shepherd that walked with a limp from an accident as a puppy. Daisy, a lean black and white mix of too many breeds to identify, waited quietly except for the sound of tails padded against the floor. I made my way to the kitchen and grabbed several meaty treats from a container. I broke them into pieces and dispersed them amongst my dogs as they performed various tricks.

"Good boys," I cooed in a voice far more juvenile than normal. "And girl," I added with a wink aimed at Daisy. Her spotted tail fluttered in delight.

A quick glance at the clock was a reminder of how late it had gotten. It was well past eleven o'clock and I needed to be in the office tomorrow morning. One more day of work and then the weekend would give me the opportunity to indulge in some of my other plans. I sighed loudly and patted Daisy absently.

"I guess it's time for bed, pups." I breathed tiredly as all four canines jumped up in an unrehearsed routine and trotted toward my room. They were incredibly obedient and would do anything I asked of them, but I allowed them to sleep on the bed alongside me. They seemed to love it and I didn't mind their show of devotion.

It was ironic how someone as evil as I could find solace in creatures as gentle as dogs, but I was not psychotic enough to wish any harm upon them. Dogs were not people. People are tainted, cruel beings that play upon my lust for blood, but dogs are different. They are only motivated by two things: food and attention. Because of that detail alone, I could never hurt them. Most people, on the other hand, are easy to kill. They reek of impure motives and it's easy to draw pleasure from their deaths. If I felt an animal was at the mercy of others, then it would be unfair to eliminate. The oppressors, however, do not receive so much care.

As I dressed appropriately for bed, a low bark sounded. I rushed out of the connecting master bathroom to find one of the dogs signaling the presence of a new sound, while the others angled their ears at the unfamiliar tune. With a smirk, my heartbeat resumed its normal rhythm as I calmed down. There was no danger. It was just the new ringtone I had set for whenever Stella called. The last time she was with me, she thought it would be so funny to change her ringtone to that of something less generic. Somehow, she convinced me to allow the tune of jingle bells, barked by a chorus of dogs, to be her personal ringtone. In hindsight, having a melody of woofs was not the best idea with four guard dogs trained to snuff out any suspicious sounds. Still, I admitted it was an amusing sight to see all of the powerful canines tilting their heads in uncertainty over a parody of a Christmas song. I waltzed over and snatched my phone from the counter. I noticed an immediate retraction of raised fur on all of my pets as the noise ceased.

"Hello," I answered in a bored tone. As much as I enjoyed all of my little sister's calls, she had no sense of boundaries. While she might be free to chat at midnight, I did have my own life. Sleep, in particular, was something this conversation would cost.

"Sylas!" an unusually cheery voice responded, "About time you picked up your phone!"

"It's almost twelve o'clock–you are lucky I answered at all."

If the giggle that echoed over the line was any indication, Stella was intoxicated. She was only twenty-two–five years younger than I–and while she wasn't very fond of alcohol, special occasions prohibited her drinking. Whatever it was she was going to say was either very good or bad.

"Don't be a baby. I come with good news!" I could almost hear her uncharacteristic smile through the phone.

"What is it?" I asked while suppressing a grumble that worked its way up my throat. If it was something that excited her, the least I could do was hide my irritation and tiredness.

"Well," she began. "Do you remember three years ago when…?"

"Dad was killed," I interjected when she seemed to have trouble forming the words.

"Yeah," she croaked in agreement with a noticeable tremor in her voice. While she had remained stoic throughout the chaotic mess of events, I knew that his death had affected her deeply. Stella was very close with our father. I never was. He was a kind, generous man who worked hard to assure the happiness of his family. While I should have swooned over having the ideal father, love was not an emotion I associated with him. I was wired differently from the start and certain passions would forever remain impossible. While I could tell Stella about my feelings of loss, it was simply not true. As monstrous as it was to admit, I was glad my father was dead. Ever since I was little, murderous thoughts had plagued my dreams and I had fought to keep those homicidal tendencies at bay. The first subject of Cain's murderous desires had been toward my father. Despite my dad's caring nature, I couldn't help but fantasize his throat slit and oozing blood. I couldn't, however, bring myself to actually do such a thing. As much as I wanted to, I knew it would have its repercussions. My innocent little sister, for starters, would have been devastated and I didn't want to cause her any pain. Stella was like the woman whose phone I had left a message on in the sense that anything directly attached to her left me feeling conflicted. I wanted to protect them. So, when I found out from a sobbing mother nearly three years ago that my father had been killed, I felt nothing but relief. Relief that I was not the one to kill him, and relief that his murder provided an opportunity. When I took the life of the bastard who had caused the family drama, it provided an excuse. Because it was my first kill, the chances of me messing up were more likely. On the fluke that I did screw up and someone like Stella managed to find out, they would be more accepting. Killing for revenge is less horrifying than killing indifferently for pleasure.

"What about it?" I probed, bringing my mind back to the conversation at hand.

"Do you remember the investigation the police did?"

"Every detail," I answered grimly.

"Remember when I said I had a feeling about that one suspect, Charles Gravo?"

I stiffened when she repeated the name of my first victim. I was suddenly intent to find out where she was going with this. Though the police had never been able to find our father's killer, they had created a list of suspects. Charles Gravo, of course, was on that list. While they had left the case inconclusive, Stella had pleaded with them to arrest Gravo. She had said she felt something was wrong with him and was suspicious. She suspected he was the one who had killed our father. When I looked into it again a few months ago, I was able to confirm her gut feeling. While I had never told her what I found out, I doubt she ever forgot him. She never let things go and I'm sure she continued to curse his name even today.

"Gravo," I sneered in repetition. I figured anger was a good reaction to go with.

She let out a cynical laugh. "You're gonna love this, then." She paused as I waited for her to continue. "I just heard the news that he was found dead in his apartment. His throat was cut wide open."

"Whoa," I said in fake shock.

"I know right!"

"Do they have any idea who was responsible?"

"I wish! I would thank whoever did it. Gotta love karma." Her drunken state was making her say a variety of other colorful phrases as well, but I knew that this conversation would be much more serious if she were sober. While she would be happ that the person who killed our father received justice , she would not be as thrilled about the method of execution.

"I guess his past caught up with him. If he really was the bad guy we thought he was then certainly dad was not his only victim," I offered.

"Yup," she agreed with a yawn. Apparently, her

personal party was winding down. "It's nice just knowing he's not out there anymore. No one else will be hurt now…" her voice lowered and tiredness oozed into her words.

It would be best to end our talk now, "It's getting a bit late, Stell. I have to be in the office tomorrow morning, but it was nice to talk to you."

"You really should call more, bro."

"I will, I promise," I said to wrap up the call. Before she could respond, I hung up.

With a heavy sigh, I eased my way back into the large, expensive furnished bedroom and sat on the bed. Accompanied by four furry beasts, I slipped into a peaceful slumber.

The house was still, apart from the blared sounds that radiated from my alarm clock. With a heavy hand, I slammed the silence button. I peeled back the soft, warm comforter and proceeded into the dark morning. Even with the heaters on full blast, the upcoming winter seeped into my large estate and left me chilled. I shrugged on a robe and headed to the bathroom to prepare for the day.

All my dogs, except for the ever-alert Daisy remained and snored in the nest of covers. She sat at my feet, her tail pounded a furious rhythm against the floor and her tongue panted out of her mouth with a smile. Unlike the others who basked in the morning, it was routine for her to follow me at whatever time I awoke. I cocked an eyebrow at the protective canine.

"Do you ever sleep?" I asked, aware that the mutt would not understand. She tilted her head and her erect ears bounced to the side. I shook my head. Of course, the dog rescued by mere coincidence with the least amount of training would be the most reliable of the bunch. While any of my companions would leap into danger to protect me, the small herder had the best reflexes.

I had a unique connection with my animals. While I struggled to create emotional attachment, the dogs were one of the few things I would admit to missing if anything happened to them. They were undoubtedly loyal and affectionate creatures without all the horrible associations humans created. *Dogs are great. They are one of the few animals who can tolerate my existence. Cats, on the other hand, hate me. I have never heard a cat purr around me; they only hiss and growl.* Even the red tabby I had grown up with despised me. The plump feline had loved attention from everyone but me. Dogs would treat you according to how you treated them, while cats acted around you always depended on who you were as a person. Cats were too smart to love someone as sinister as me, but the unconditional love of a dog never failed.

28

After I showered, groomed, and dressed, I marched into the spacious living room. Grabbing four silver dishes from the floor, I filled them with a mix of dry kibble and fresh meat. Spoiled mutts had a better diet than I did! I didn't even have to call the dogs for their breakfast. They were all perfectly aware when it was time to eat. I barked out a few commands before allowing them access to their food. A few sit, stay, wait, and okays later, the sound of the munching beasts echoed throughout the house.

I passed by the mirror one more time to assure that I was in top shape. My tailored dark grey suit sat eloquently on my healthy frame, but I still brushed over the shoulders self-consciously. I filtered my fingers through my bright blonde hair to assure that it was shaped in the most professional way possible before I grabbed my keys, laptop, and then headed out the door. The dogs would be fine on their own. A doggy door in the back fed into all six acres of land while a custom electric fence safely enclosed them in their huge backyard.

The slow drive into the city was smooth and I found myself immersed in thoughts about the future. Instead of looking for another victim to kill, this weekend would be filled with something that I was far more interested in. A charity event hosted by a church was going on and I fully intended to be there. The woman who had witnessed my first kill just so happened to be a volunteer. I had already left the message on her phone and I always kept my promises. I would indeed see her soon, except this time I would not allow her to escape. No, I decided that I would keep her until I made up my mind about what to do.

I found that my shoulders felt lighter as I worked through the endless stream of conferences and papers. Being the young CEO of a major firm was no joke and while I was always swamped with work, today felt easier. All of the killing and the anticipation of capturing my next victim left me feeling better than I ever had been. While I bubbled with excitement over the next life I would take, the time in-between suddenly felt more fulfilled. Cain, a part of me that had craved for so long, was finally being fed. Even though I would have to hunt again soon, the lion was content with his offerings.

At one point during the day, one of the menial workers had noticed my unnatural smile.

"You seem a lot happier lately," the short statured man commented while he itched at the collar of his button down. He was brave to talk to someone so much higher on the food chain than himself and I rewarded him with a bright smile.

"Ah, yes. I've recently taken up a new hobby," I admitted jokingly before I headed back to my office.

When I finally had a moment alone I whipped out my phone. I went to the photos I had recently saved until I found the picture I was looking for. Piper Rowan may have made all her social media accounts private–and I wouldn't risk friending her or anything–but I was able to pull an image of her off Google. The picture was a selfie she had taken a few weeks prior to the incident. While she looked pretty in the photo with her dark curls flowed down her shoulders and chocolate eyes dazzled for the camera, something seemed off. The picture did not do her justice. Instead, it made her appear normal, like everyone else. I could easily kill anyone else. I was disappointed because she had to be special. I wasn't able to force my hands to finish her off and that frightened me. There had to be something different about her. As much as I admired the picture I needed to see her for myself. The picture made her look like a normal person. But to me, all normal people were corrupted and, henceforth, prey. I didn't want her to be prey though. I wanted a way to silence Cain. The image of her only caused doubt to form a pit in my stomach, but I would know the truth soon enough. If I found her on Saturday and it turned out it was all a fluke, I would kill her. As simple as that. If she really was all I chalked her up to be in my head, then she wasn't going anywhere.

The day flew by quickly and before I knew it, the sun had set. I was working later today to try to get as much done as I could before the weekend. I needed to be distraction free for a few days and I was tying up as many loose ends as possible. Before exiting the office, I called in my personal assistant.

Jared, much like me, had a knack for numbers and a brilliant memory. He was able to organize and remember my schedule with ease. Had the young intern not been so infatuated with planning, he would have done wonderfully in the field of math. I had even approached him with the idea of training to be one of my accountants, but he had declined. I thought it was a waste of talent, but the boy seemed content fetching supplies and looking at calendars.

He met me moments after I demanded his presence.

"Yes sir," the copper haired PA said while fidgeting in his semi-formal attire. The young man was thin and lanky and barely fit into any of the oversized polos he wore.

"I wanted to remind you that my vacation is coming up this week and I will not be available from Saturday onward. I'll have my phone on me but I'd prefer to not have to use it," I stared at him. It wasn't unusual for me to go on vacation, despite my reputation for working constantly. I was invested in the company I brought to fame, but that didn't mean I never stopped working. I did have a solid work ethic and a great level of devotion, but I was always keen to rest for a little while. There was more to life than work. *Like killing.*

He nudged his large glasses up his nose, "Of course. I've made sure that your emails and calls will be attended to. Anything else?"

"Sounds great. Thanks, Jared," I spoke. "And here," I handed him the Sudoku puzzle from the newspaper. He loved numbers, and it was interesting to see how quickly he could solve each puzzle. It wasn't much, but the gesture was my way of paying him back for an especially hectic week.

"Thanks!" He scratched at his neck and my gaze instantly went to his throat. While I valued his usefulness, I still had to restrain myself from killing him. With no one else around and my attention focused on the vital artery that currently thrummed against his skin, it was hard to tame Cain from a potential strike. All I wanted to do was grab the nearest sharp object and force it into his flesh with a pop and watch the blood squirt out in rapid beats.

I pinched the bridge of my nose and turned away. *NO! DON'T DO IT!*

My conscious mind screamed against Cain.

"Alright, see you when I return then," it took every ounce of strength to keep my voice regulated. While I despised all people, including him, he made a great assistant and I would—admittedly– miss his presence. It would be such a hassle to replace him with someone competent enough to function at the rate I required. I could kill him in a heartbeat, but there were people I needed less, that would do just as well to serve up to Cain.

I marched through the sky scraped building, to the elevators, and to my car. The drive home was quiet, as usual. I preferred to not listen to music in the car, for I found it distracting. I would much rather have my thoughts wander through the empty vehicle. As I opened my mind, all I could think about was tomorrow. I was excited to see her again, but also nervous. Murder was easier than kidnapping; once you were done, you simply had to dispose the body, but kidnapping required maintaining a live subject. Other than my dogs, I had never been responsible for another being. The logical side of me knew that this was crazy and had too much potential to go wrong, but another part of me felt that this had to happen.

****

Saturday arrived at last. The hours leading up to the plan were tedious as my anticipation grew. I was nearly shaking as I prepared for the event. I adjusted my tie into place and cracked my knuckles. It was now or never. Time to follow up on an old friend. I looked at the swarm of dogs at my feet.

"We might be having a guest later," I informed the clueless fluff balls. "Alright, I'm off now, pups. Wish me luck," I winked and exited my home and entered the garage. I didn't bother to enter the address into the GPS. I had studied the area on Google maps to be sure that I knew every route like the back of my hand. Although there was no guide to kidnapping, I assumed it was a rule that knowing the territory would make it a lot easier.

Before I went through with everything, I needed to take care of Cain's request. While I hoped to be able to kill the intriguing witness, there was no guarantee it would be that easy and would require my full attention. As I watched her every move, it would be impossible to attend to anything else. With a deep- seated need for blood, quickly moved me into an exhilarated state, there was one thing I needed to do before I captured *her*.

I made a quick stop near a dimly populated area. It was not too far from my future destination and I was certain there would be someone there that could be of assistance. Graffiti littered the old and crumbled buildings. In the distance, a series of small houses sat. The rugged concrete scraped along the soles of my black dress shoes. The clothing I had worn was quite formal, but with good reason. It was unlikely that my prey would recognize me in my current state. The silken button-down shirt and coat I donned were vastly different from the scraggly threads I'd worn upon our first encounter. Piper would have to be looking for me to notice, but I assumed she would be too distracted to fully examine my facial features. My clothing, in that sense, would serve as a makeshift disguise. It gifted me with the aspect of surprise. It did, however, make me stick out in the context of an informal gathering. I would bide my time quietly until the opportunity to speak with her arose naturally.

I ducked behind a rundown building when a flash of movement captured my gaze. Hidden by the large structure's shadow, a woman clads in dark attire strode slowly as she counted the money in her hands. A smaller form retreated away from her until it was out of sight. With a gun slung to the side of the stout woman, it was not hard to guess what had just transpired.

I slithered toward the unaware robber like a snake. As I popped in front of her, I flashed my white teeth. She jumped at my sudden appearance and her hand flew to her side.

Not wanting her to get ahold of the weapon holstered at her waist, I darted closer and blocked her arm with my own. I grabbed the lethal device for myself and raised it above her short head. With her free hand, she scratched at my arm, but I remained unfazed and retained my hold of the gun.

"Give that back," she demanded. Despite her youthful vigor, she appeared to be in her thirties, and the deep lines around her eyes told of a difficult life.

"Guns are for cowards," I corrected condescendingly. Guns were incredibly powerful and while they had their use, I still preferred the thrill of the hand-to-hand dance. There was no way to avoid being close to your victims with a blade, but a gun offered a longer range. It added distance, which is why I never used such a weak weapon. Relying on something else to do all the work, took all the fun away from the kill. If I wanted to feel the power as people bled from my hands, then it would be only that; at *my* hands. To remove that control would make things too easy.

She charged at me and I barely lunged to the side in time to evade collision. She dropped the cash in her hand and used both hands to strike. I tried to dodge, but she was faster than I had thought and was rewarded with a feathered blow to my side. When I noticed her aiming at a place much lower and more sensitive, I decided it was time to finish this.

Flicking the safety on, I tossed the gun behind me and grabbed hold of the feisty woman. With my hand around her throat, I pinned her to the wall. The bricks scraped against my fingers as I held her in place.

With a gasp she sputtered, "What do you want from me?"

My intentions were obviously to kill her, but I had something else on my mind too. This was the first time I had interacted with another criminal because the first man I killed didn't count. She might not have killed, but there could be more about her that I couldn't see.

"Did you steal from those people?" I asked. I couldn't care less what her answer was, as it didn't matter in any sense. I didn't differentiate between those who were morally just and those that were not. For me; prey was prey. I just wanted to see what I could learn from this woman before I ultimately erased her from the world.

She shook her head violently against my tight grasp. She was heavy and it took both hands to support her weight from her neck without completely crushing the delicate windpipe.

I jerked my head in the direction of the gun scattered a few feet away on the ground, "I'd appreciate some honesty."

She avoided my harsh gaze. When our eyes reconnected, I noticed tears obscuring her dark irises. "I had no choice," she pleaded sadly. She looked regretful at the cash spilled on the ground below and I deflated in disappointment.

The person I held up against the wall was troubled, but

ordinary. A small part of me had hoped the opposite had been true. For a split second, I thought I had finally found my kin. I was excited to meet someone else with an inner darkness similar to Cain, to prove that I was not the only one of the non- conformed. I needed something to prove I was not alone but, instead, my existence as an outlier proved to be once again.

I dropped my hands from her thick dermis. She fell to the ground with an audible thud. Before she managed to regain her balance and got on her feet again, I kicked her back down. She squealed at the forceful blow.

"If you had no choice then neither do I," I rasped while unsheathing the small blade I kept handy in the pocket of my jacket. In one foul swoop, I managed to swipe deep into the vital flesh before I retreated with a hop.

I stood back and watched the life drain out of her from afar. I didn't want to get anything on me that would mar my clean appearance. I would be going in public soon after and I hadn't thought to bring a spare outfit.

When the flow of blood began to stop and the red puddle no longer grew in size, I turned and picked the gun from the ground. I swept over it with the inner sleeves of my dark suit to get rid of any fingerprints before I tossed it to lie beside its dead owner.

As I walked away from the scene, I couldn't help but feel glum. Granted, the endorphins from the kill coursed through my system and provided a physical euphoria, but mental distractions prevented me from embracing the full sense of gratification. The bloodshed by my hands caused a radiation of power from my pores. Engulfed in ecstasy, I should have been satisfied, but something still tugged in the back of my mind. The woman I left in the puddle of her own blood had no murderous intentions toward the people she had robbed. She had stolen but, from the distress and exhaustion on her face, it was not for a malicious reason. It bugged me. Maybe I had hoped to see someone else capable of the same atrocities I committed daily.

As I climbed into my car with an undisturbed walk back, the thought continued to flutter around my mind. I liked the idea of discovering someone else as evil as me, but I wondered if it was impossible. Maybe I was alone, with only Cain to keep me company in this tainted world. Hopefully, though, my plan for today would remedy that. My heart thumped rapidly as I drove to the place that would begin the next stage of Cain's demonic tendencies.

I pulled into the parking spot I had chosen and smiled. It was perfect. At the edge of the park, surrounded by trees to provide cover, but not too far away from the event; it was the perfect place. Without witnesses or cameras, it was just the place I had been looking for.

I exited the car and walked casually toward the crowded park. Small booths lined the entire walkway. A variety of vendors had set up small exhibits and handed out small items to the mass of people that moved through the park.

I immersed myself into the herd of people and cruised through the section, until I came across the target of my search. A small booth that advertised a local church was last in its row. As I eased my way through the human flood, I spotted her. In a red long-sleeved T-shirt which read the name of her church on the front and a pair of dark jeans; she mulled around and answered questions. Even with her long, dark hair pulled into a tight bun; it was unmistakably her.

As I mustered the strength, I replayed my routine. I had rehearsed lines back and forth in rapid succession. I was ready. Instead of going to the front of the booth, I slithered around back. I strode forward until I was just inches away before I prodded at her shoulder with my finger.

"Excuse me, miss," I said in a falsely, innocent southern drawl.

"What can I do for you, sir?" she asked as she turned around. Her face was aimed in my direction, but I made sure she didn't really see me. I avoided eye contact and had my head tilted at an angle to avoid any premature recognition.

"Well, you see, this is a bit awkward," I said with hand gestures and closed eyes to add to the effect of awkwardness. "It would appear my wife is having a bit of womanly trouble," I coughed appropriately, "You wouldn't happen to have any extra monthly female supplies, would you?"

She blushed. "Oh, um well…yes, I guess so. Where is she?"

"She is a bit too flustered to leave the car if you wouldn't mind," I said as I set the bait that I half expected her to refuse. If this ploy didn't work I had plans to come back later even if it would be inconvenient.

She nodded slowly, "Okay. Just hold on one second," I backed away out of sight just in time for her to inform the other person in the booth that she would be right back. As soon as she left her little exhibit, she was mine. I had lured her out of her safety zone and every step closer to the car lowered her chance of escape.

When we finally arrived at the spot where I had parked, she did a double take. She looked through the windows of the empty vehicle suspiciously before she turned back to me. The alarm in her soft brown eyes was visible as she met my gaze. She paused as if trying to place who I was. I was in my usual formal clothes–a suit and tie–and looked very different from that time I wore rags on our first encounter. Her thin eyebrow raised as recognition dawned, but was still out of reach.

Since I figured that I had her now, I went ahead and revealed my identity in a way she would remember. I walked toward her and she backed up until her back hit the car. I placed my hands by her sides on the car so that she was trapped. I exhaled.

"Didn't you get my message, Piper?"

Chapter 4

I stared deeply into those harsh blue eyes that seemed locked on me. I knew those icy hues. They belonged to the madman that had haunted my dreams. *How did he find me?* I knew he most likely did some browsing on my phone, hence the reason I had stayed away from the public eye for a while, and I figured I would be safe. I had signed up to volunteer weeks in advance and I didn't want to abandon the job. I also figured that being surrounded by a group of people would protect me from him. Of course, safety in numbers didn't work when I was stupid enough to wander away for some awkward request.

I looked around, my eyes scanned my surroundings. My back was pressed to the cold metal of his car and his hands pinned me to the spot. We were alone in a pack of trees and the area of the park where I had previously been just out of my sight range. This was bad. I had to get away. There was no telling what he would do to me once he managed to get me even further away from the safety of people.

I ducked under his arms and started to dash away. Before I could cover any ground, a tug at the collar of my shirt brought me to a standstill. He managed to snake his other hand around and covered my mouth quicker than I could scream. My words were trapped under his warm hand. I squirmed desperately and kicked backward. One of my hits landed near his groin and he grunted, but managed to maintain his tight grasp.

The next thing I knew, the world spun and darkened. Chloroform. Real classy.

I woke up dazed and unable to see anything. I was about to freak out over my temporary blindness when I realized I was in literal darkness. The scratchy carpeted floor on which I rested, paired with the rocky vibrations from the road, alerted me to the fact that I was in a trunk. My head pounded and I wanted nothing more than to close my eyes and pretend I was elsewhere, but I had to stay awake. If the car still moved, that meant we hadn't reached our destination yet. There was still time. I tried to bring my arms forward only to realize that, like my legs, they were bound together with duct tape. I was also gagged and every small movement left my muscles protesting. It would appear, I wouldn't be able to easily slip out of this car in my current condition.

Taking a deep breath, I did my best to relax my erratic

heartbeat. I should have been hopped on adrenalin, but being drugged had really messed with my senses. As I tried to calm down, I noticed a slight glint. Only the smallest fraction of light penetrated the dark space, but enough to reflect off my necklace. If my hands weren't stuck behind my back, I would have grabbed the golden cross on its chain and properly valued the comfort it provided. The accessory had been a gift from my mother when I was young and I had treasured it ever since. Maybe it was a sign that not all hope was lost. Maybe I could make it out of this unscathed.

Of course, Arial! I thought about how my friend would find me. She was supposed to pick me up after the event and she would note my absence. She would call the police and they would find me before it was too late. The small flame of hope that burst to life was extinguished as soon as realization hit. Like a splash of cold water, I quickly understood it would not be that easy. The man who had taken me had asked for my assistance unnoticed and with the flood of people at the event, no one would remember him enough to even provide a description. To make matters worse, I could feel that my pocket was empty, so there would be no way to track my phone. Today was not my day.

I wanted to bang on the hood and scream until someone could hear me, but knew it would be futile. The car moved steadily and, at the pace we were going, much too fast for any hostage like me to attract any attention. Instead, I squirmed around until I was in a position where my feet were faced; what I assumed was where the door opened. When he tried to get me out of there, I would return the favor for drugging and kidnapping me. It was very uncomfortable as I had to scrunch my body into a tight ball and the bindings on my limbs didn't help, but it would be worth it. Even if I didn't make it out of this alive, I would go down knowing that I inflicted some pain.

I shook my head. This wasn't me. I spread thoughts of love and peace and was opposed to any type of violence. It was how I was raised. In this situation, however, normal rules didn't apply. If it meant going against my beliefs to stop this crazed man and prevented him from hurting any more innocent people, then I would do what needed to be done. It didn't hurt that my initial retaliation in the form of a kick to the gut wouldn't suck either. I wasn't perfect and I admitted that. I too experienced some anger and wouldn't mind if I took it out on the sociopath on the other end of the car.

When the car slowed down and took a turn onto what seemed to be a less inhabited road, I knew we were there. The car came to a smooth stop along the, what I presumed to be, dirt road. The plush interior of the trunk blocked out most noise, but I thought I heard the sound of dogs barking in the distance. The engine silenced and the rickety vibrations along my back ceased as the car shuddered once and then fell quiet. Without the added noise, I was aware of the thuds that signaled my kidnapper's approach. I brought my knees as close to my chest as they could; my muscles coiled and ready to spring despite the debilitating restraints.

At last, rays of light flooded my widened pupils and I was blinded by the sudden illumination. Although I wasn't able to see, I had a basic idea of where he might be and I launched myself at him in a haze of kicks and flailed limbs. I must have caught him by surprise as I felt my feet collide with solid muscle. He stumbled back with a hiss, but recovered and managed to grab ahold of me. By the time he grabbed me, though, I had managed to wiggle out through the open door and onto the driveway. I lashed my tied limbs out furiously and mumbled underneath the gag, but he managed to dodge the other blows that flew his way. He grabbed me by the stomach and turned me around until my back was flush against his chest. My arms were tied in front of me and I wasn't able to kick back far enough to do any damage. As ferocious as I tried to be, with all the bindings and the way he held me, I only managed to flail helplessly. I continued with my barrage of attacks until I felt my energy dwindle and relaxed against him in surrender. He didn't move. He just held me there.

I squinted my eyes through the tears that flowed freely and looked around. Trees stretched on endlessly to the horizon uninterrupted except for the large clearing ahead. We were in the middle of nowhere. Feet planted firmly on the gravel path where we stood, I continued to crane my head from side to side in the hopes of finding other signs of life. Of course, to my dismay, there weren't any. It was just us. This was where he had made his home, but no one else had and we were alone in this endless chunk of nature. I was usually very outdoorsy and, on any other occasion, I would have found the untainted land beautiful. The mini forest wasn't the only striking thing though. When I finally laid eyes upon what I assumed was his home, my jaw would had dropped had it not already been occupied with a gag. I was not looking at a house but rather, a mansion. It was huge! The sleek, modern, estate, though only one-story, was massive. The only thing my middle-class brain could compare it to in terms of size was a large chain store, like Walmart or Target.

Then it hit me. I glanced back to see the shiny BMW that had just transported me here and also felt the silky fibers of my attacker's obviously expensive suit when the pieces clicked. Whoever this guy was, he was very wealthy. That meant he was not just a common criminal. He was *somebody* and that meant whatever power he held would now be turned against mine.

"Welcome home," the familiar voice from my nightmares whispered in my ear. He pulled me into the garage and with the flick of a switch, the door to the outside world closed and I was alone with the monster in his territory. He moved a hand up to my gag while still maintained a firm hold on my abdomen. As he began to remove it he said, "You can scream if you want, but try not to scare the dogs, okay?"

As soon as the cloth was gently lifted from my mouth, I let out pierced scream that I knew my throat would be sore. It wasn't a scream made to signal help, but a wail of despair. Something bad would happen and there would be nothing I could do to stop it. I turned my head at an angle so that I could see his face. I expected him to be smiling sadistically at the pathetic cries of his prey, but instead he studied me with a frown.

"Better?" he asked.

I looked straight ahead again and grunted. He didn't deserve anything more. If he fed off the anguish of others, my scream was the only thing he would get. I would remain stoic. Taking a deep breath, I urged the tears to stop. I would not cry anymore in front of this beast. I was numb as he carried me into the house. My limbs refused to work, and I was forcibly dragged into the extravagant dwelling. I couldn't even gawk at the lush home through my state of paralyzed terror.

I was barely cognizant as he led me into what looked like a kitchen furnished for an expert chef. Beautiful granite countertops stretched for miles and barstools lined the edges. From the other side of the humongous house some unsettled animals let loose a various array of noises. He had mentioned dogs so I assumed that those were the creatures that whined and howled desperately. Despite the noise, they didn't come running toward us as I expected them to. Dogs usually greeted their owners, or so I had heard.

As if he could read my thoughts, the man whose arms were wrapped around me said, "My pups are well trained. You'll meet them soon enough but not yet," His grip tightened as if he feared I would struggle.

He was wrong if he believed I would continue to fight him. The drug he had exposed me to earlier, plus all of my fighting, had left me physically drained. If I had any chance of escape, I would need all my strength. My shoulders sagged and eyes fluttered.

Suddenly, his hands lost purchase and he released me. With no strength remaining, I slipped to the floor.

"Whoa there," he exclaimed as he managed to snag me before my face could plant onto the cold floor.

"What do you want with me?" I asked desperately. I sank

down on my knees and he followed suit and crouched down by my side.

"I was hoping you could help me figure that out," he admitted with a shrug.

Despite my fatigue, renewed anger almost had me lashing out again. He had kidnapped me, caused a great ordeal of stress, for a reason that he himself had ye to find. "You are a murderer," I spat.

A blonde eyebrow arched up in response. "How so?"

"I saw you kill that poor old man! Don't you dare deny it!" I all but screamed at him.

Thin, pink lips twitched at the corners, "Well, you got me there," he admitted humorously. "If it makes you feel any better, that guy was no innocent."

"There is no justification for killing someone! Some people are less innocent than others, but it's not your job to decide how they will pay for their sins!"

He eyed me necklace warily. I expected him to make some snide comment about my beliefs, but he held his tongue. Raising his hands in surrender he commented, "We are not going to get anywhere chatting here on the floor, let's get you someplace cozier."

"I would be coziest in my own home."

What home?" That apartment you abandoned or the place you were staying with that friend of yours?"

I gasped. Since finding the message on my phone; it was obvious he had discovered my apartment, but there was no way he could have found where Arial lived, let alone the fact that I was staying with her for the time being.

"How did y—" I started. He swept his hand in a motion that emphasized the space we were in.

"Look around," he ordered gently. I didn't see anything beside the fancy furnishings and extravagant décor. He caught on to my confusion and quickly clarified, "I have money and power," He laughed, "Enough connections and determination too as I seem to know a lot about you, Piper Rowan."

I cringed at his mention of my full name, "But why?" He shrugged, "Curiosity."

"Curiosity killed the cat, you know," I retorted on cue with a cliché.

"I hate cats," He stood up in one fluid motion and grabbed my arm to pull me along with him.

I made no protest and was in a state of shock as he swept me through the long hallway and led us into a room at the end of the corridor. I assumed from sheer size of the room that it must have been the master suite, but the absence of any furniture made it clear that it was nothing more than a guest space. Unlike the main sections of the house, the room had plush white carpet that absorbed the weight of my feet. It also deviated from the black and white color scheme of the rest of the estate with its dark blue walls.

There was a small window on the wall opposite the door. It brightened up the room to the point where it was comfortable, despite the overhead lights off. I was just beginning to wonder why he would risk leaving me alone in a room with a possible escape when I realized that the window was set in its frame. It was a porthole made to allow a view into an abyss that was so close, yet forbidden. While I didn't dismiss the idea of knocking it in right away, I knew that it would be reinforced with more than just a thin layer of glass and with nothing else present that could add weight.

I tugged my arm back into place and was a bit relieved to find that he hadn't fought to maintain his grasp. Granted, it meant that he was confident enough that I couldn't slip away and escape. *What exactly am I trying to escape from?* I had yet to find anything about my attacker and who knew what his curiosity would lead to. Either way, there was no chance I would get out of this unscathed.

My attention was brought back at the low click of a lock. I swung my head away from the window to see that I was alone and the door was closed behind me. Whatever was coming, would have to wait. For now, I was locked in a prison where even my worst fears couldn't predict what would happen.

Chapter 5

I paced up and down the hallway restlessly as I relived the past few hours in my head. What had I done this time? I couldn't believe I had actually done it. I had stolen her away and locked her in my home. Unlike before though, this had crossed a line. My kills had thus far been quick and precise with the purpose of fulfilling Cain's desires. Kidnapping her was neither fast, nor purposeful. It was selfish.

I scrubbed a shaky hand through my slick hair and made a feral noise that was halfway between a growl and a sigh of frustration. I shouldn't have bothered fulfilling this silly quest. Did I really think she would be able to provide the answers I seek? At the time of my first kill I had been unable to finish her off properly. Inexperienced and caught off guard, my confidence had been shaken. It was just a momentary hesitation that I assured myself would not happen again. Rejuvenated with the thought that it was some mere mishap that had allowed this witness to escape the first time, I dashed to the kitchen and retrieved the one thing that could make up for this error.

I removed my jacket, unbuttoned the cuffs, and rolled the sleeves up to my elbows. There was no sense in getting my clothes stained. Knife in hand, I slithered down the hall with renewed purpose. The familiar excitement rattled in my gut as Cain's thirst salivated at the thought of his next kill. There was another feeling mixed in there too, but I couldn't quite put my finger on the feeling. The hallway seemed endless as my bloodlust reached its climax. I needed to feel the blood flow across my hands immediately or I would be overtaken by Cain. As I opened the door, it was all I could do to refrain from charging inside and slashing her to pieces. I knew the position and depth of the jugular so intimately that I knew exactly how much pressure it took to reach it with the blade that was tightly encased in my fingers.

She faced the window when I entered. The lock made an audible click and there was no way she could have missed the sound. Her back to me was an act of defiance. I cleared my throat to make clear that I wanted my presence acknowledged. I loved to look into the eyes as the life drained from my victims. It was something so unique to watch as the small organs unfocused as their owner ceased to exist. It was so curious how one deep look into the eyes could identify whether or not someone was alive. There was no immediate change to them but somehow, I could always tell. Maybe it was a separate sense that allowed us to feel that spark of connection that was absent in blindness. When the connection in the gaze between my victim and I severed, despite them never looking away, I knew their reign of life had ended. It was such a thrill to be the one who caused other's stares to deaden.

Maybe that's why I needed her to turn around and face me so much. I needed to look at her when I ended things. It fed Cain's appetite, or it had done so before. When she finally turned around, however, it was not what I expected. The unidentified emotion from earlier was made obvious. Dread.

The moment her beautiful brown irises zoned in on me, I felt the urge to drop my weapon. *What the hell?* Although it went against my bizarre feelings, I pulled my focus into place and tried to revert back to Cain's instincts that had been there just moments before. Try as I might, I couldn't tempt Cain back to the surface and the desire for death that had been unbearable before I entered the room, had disappeared entirely. The last thing I wanted to do was hurt her. It would be like putting a dog down. *A dog! That's exactly what it was!*

I began to laugh hysterically as I pinpointed what it was that had bothered me. I was so caught up in my own mind, I almost failed to notice the way her slender form bunched up as her muscles coiled and released. I stuck my arm out, but it was too late. She sprung past me and slipped out of the room.

I let out a spring of curses as I dashed after her. I was fast, but with a head start and the determination of someone with their life on the line, she managed to stay out of reach. She sprinted past the hallway and was getting awfully close to the door that led to the porch. If she managed to get there, she could take off into the woods. A pursuit through the trees in the darkening evening was not ideal and my mind spun with ways to stop her when I finally thought of the answer.

I whistled as loudly as I could manage and yelled, "Daisy, come!"

In a flurry of paws and fluff, the black and white herding mix flew in from the doggy door just in time to prevent my victim's escape. She froze with confusion, just long enough for me to get closer. When she realized what had happened, she tried to change her trajectory and ran away from her cornered position, but my loyal canine had done her job and I grabbed her arm. She twisted and pushed back with enough force that I lost my balance. I refused to let go, though, and she stumbled toward the cold marble floors with me. Not wanting to accidentally crush my unsuspecting pet, I angled myself as I fell so I would not hurt my precious dog.

My back hit the hard surface with such power that I swore my vertebrae jarred around. I, however achy from my collision with the floor, did not relent my grip and wrapped my arm around her midsection.

She wasn't willing to give up either and in a tangle of limbs, we rolled around. Luckily, my larger size proved to be advantageous as I managed to reverse positions so that I ended on top. Hovering over her small form, I was able to subdue her beneath me. What I didn't realize, unfortunately, was the fact that I still held the knife.

As I tried to reduce her struggling, her knee connected with my ribs. With the air knocked out of me, I gasped. The useless flailing of her arms changed into something fiercer, the harder she tried to escape. Outstretched fingers turned into fists that hammered into my sides. She wasn't strong enough to do any real damage, but I would be covered in bruises the next day.

I grunted as I attempted to trap her arms beneath my own.

Unfortunately, she changed her position at the last moment and the blade that had been hanging harmlessly in my hand was met with resistance. Feeling her wince, I turned my head and found that my weapon had lodged in her cheek.

Red drops of hypnotizing scarlet liquid oozed out of the cut and dripped onto the floor in a mesmerizing pattern. Normally seeing the blood spill from my victims was enough to trigger the euphoria that I sought, but not this time. Instead of that pleasurable rush of chemicals, I felt my stomach knot. The unfamiliar sensation of dread lurked again.

She stilled and shut her eyes.

Somehow that simple action aggravated me to the point where I roared, "LOOK AT ME!" I was not going to accept her surrender.

She shook her head and murmured her protest.

I pulled the knife from her face and regretfully regarded the ebbing flow of blood. It was several inches in length from the edge of her cheek to her forehead. The cut wasn't deep enough to reach bone, but it was still significant enough that it would certainly leave a scar. As much as I regretted harming her, a part of me liked the idea of my mark leaving a lasting impression. It was still very likely I would find a way to kill her before this was all over, but on the slight chance that she got away; she would never be free. I traced my finger over the open flesh and a wry smirk worked its way onto my facial features as I stroked the exposed muscle in between the bleeding flaps of skin. She began to shake at my carnal curiosity and I pulled my hand away.

Something moist pressed against my forearm and I looked to the side to see Daisy watching me patiently. Instead of the usual thrumming of her tail bumping against the floor, it was silent. I pried my hands off my victim's arms to make her more comfortable, but left my lower half pressed against her to prevent any escape. Her eyes remained closed but her hand flew up and cupped her cheek. Daisy edged closer and sniffed her face.

I nodded to my curious mutt and ordered, "Daisy, out." With what looked similar to a pout, she inched away and exited out the doggy door.

Alone again, I placed my thumb and forefinger along her chin. "Piper," I said softly.

She pried her eyes open at the mention of her name. As I looked into her chocolate depths, I found that while my theory was spot on, I still didn't know why. Why did she escape my usual classification of humans that made them so easy to kill? Why did she provoke such a primitive level of protectiveness that had, before now, been reserved only for my mother, Stella, and dogs? The closest I came to caring about something used to be limited to my dogs as I would never sacrifice any of them. So why did she cause the same reaction if she obviously wasn't canine?

"Are you going to finish it?" she asked with a shaky voice. Instead of answering her I asked, "What do you think of dogs?"

Despite our strange position with blood dripping down her face, she took the time to raise her eyebrow in confusion.

"I guess that can wait until later," I suggested. I stood up and grabbed her arm to propel her up along with me. She didn't struggle and resumed that shocked state from earlier.

I dropped her in the room and locked the door as I went to retrieve a washcloth, Neosporin, and a large Band-Aid. She was sitting down on the soft carpet in the far corner of the room. I closed the door from behind, walked over, and took a seat next to her. I could tell she wanted to rebel against me as I began to clean her wound but other than the anger that flared in her eyes, there was no sign of protest as she kept to herself.

"You know what I am. I am a killer. I love watching the life drain out of my victims and the way they are at my mercy as the blood flows out of their ruptured veins and stains their corpses," her eyes widened and if she wasn't stuck in the corner, she would have tried to get more space between us. "But," I added, "you are different. For whatever reason, I'm not satisfied when your blood spills," I dabbed the cloth coated with antiseptic along her gash.

"You are the embodiment of evil," she hissed and grappled with her necklace.

"Yes," I admitted. I pulled the washcloth away and found it stained with the remaining gush of blood. For the most part, the wound had clotted and no longer oozed as it had before, "And I suppose you are the opposite, then? What, the face of benevolence?"

She shook her head, "I do not claim to be pure or perfect, but I would certainly never submit to such evil forces."

Just my luck; the one person I wanted to kill, I couldn't. She preached on behalf of goodness. It was annoying, but there was no way to permanently shut her up. I couldn't kill her, but I could scare her.

"You are evil! Who knows how many lives you have ended?" she continued.

"Four."

"What?" she questioned.

"I've killed four people," I exclaimed with a proud smile.

"That's awful! How could you commit such atrocities?" she shook her head disbelievingly, "You have hurt more than four people. Each of them has– had–a family, friends, and they too will suffer at their loss."

At this I laughed, "While I wish I could exaggerate my numbers to that extent, it's four."

She glared at me with a menace I didn't believe she had, "No, you've also brought pain to their—"

"Friends? Families?" I interrupted. "Don't be naïve. A fleeting moment of upset over a lost resource is all they will really feel. Any that say otherwise are doing such things for either sympathy or to save face. People only care about themselves."

"That is not true at all!" she protested passionately as her hands trembled at her sides.

"We all live in our own world where having others present is convenient, but in the end, all of our so-called attachments last as long as they are useful. Do you know what your life is to someone who doesn't need your help? White noise," With that, I gathered all my materials and left her alone to contemplate my words.

When the satisfactory click of the lock assured me that she would stay put, I wandered off to take care of other things. I greeted my dogs at last and rewarded them with their meals, before I went into my own room. I changed into more casual clothes–a T-shirt and shorts—and decided to go outside.

The sun must have set sometime during all the commotion

because only the stars greeted my entrance into nature. It was very cold but instead of turning back and getting a jacket, I embraced the chill slithering across my skin. I let out a white puff of air where my breath mixed with the frigid atmosphere.

I jogged through the maze of trees at a restrained pace to avoid colliding with any obstacles in the dark. The moon provided a decent amount of illumination in the clearing where my house was, but under the cover of trees; it was intensely dark. I pushed myself to keep going despite the ungainly conditions. Before long, I was accompanied by a barrage of paws that drummed against the chilly ground. My dogs loved to run around the large property especially when I accompanied them. I whistled a series of notes and was pleased when they were repeated the tune back at me. Eventually all our rhythms matched and the pounding of our steps became synched. As I increased my speed slightly, the mutts fell into step beside me and matched it easily.

After what must have been a long time, my labored breath and ached muscles made it hard to go any further. I ran slowly home, refreshed from my exertion and ready to return to the situation at hand. The run was a welcome way to escape all troublesome thoughts and gave me plenty of time to think of what I needed to accomplish. I shivered as my perspiration only added to the cold of the night. As I walked into my abode, I thought about the woman I had trapped. What was she thinking right now? I wanted to return to the room and converse with her more in hopes of solving the mystery she had become, but I knew that she needed some time on her own, so I forced myself to wait until morning.

Instead I showered, changed, and prepared for bed.

Before I fell asleep, a buzzing sound originating from my phone captured my attention. I grabbed the device from my dresser and examined it. I had a text notification from my sister.

Have fun on your vacation!

I was confused for a moment before I remembered that I had informed her, much in the way I did my work that I would be on vacation over the course of the next week. In truth, I wasn't actually going anywhere but with everything going on, I hadn't wanted to risk her dropping by on one of her surprise visits. I replied in a way that was simple and to the point.

I will.

Of course, being the technology obsessed person she was, Stella's response was immediate.

Get a tan while you're at it. Can't have everyone thinking I summon spirits cuz my bro looks like a ghost ;)

I rolled my eyes. If only she knew what I was up to, she

wouldn't had bothered with all this sibling banter. I placed my phone back on the dresser and flopped down into bed. I sunk into the warm covers while it was cozy and struggled to fall asleep. There was too much going on. I still shook with the need to kill, but the one thing that I should kill was too far out of reach. I was conflicted and had a feeling this internal struggle was only the beginning.

****

I awoke to the annoyingly familiar sound of my alarm. While I usually awoke feeling rested and ready for the day, I struggled to pry my eyes open. Sleep had been hard to achieve and when I managed to fall asleep, my dreams were plagued with graphic images. While I normally found a strange comfort in these types of horrors, I felt oddly disturbed. Considering the subject had been the female who was only a few doors away, I assumed that was the source of my conflicted emotions. The provocative images included her being manhandled and killed by my own two hands. I should have been relieved. Maybe, if I started to think about killing her, I could finally be rid of this witness; the bump in the road, but something was off. For whatever reason, I was bothered by the thought of her death.

I ground the palm of my hand against my forehead as I forced my way out of bed. Cain wasn't complicated, but she was. The growl emanating from my stomach was a reminder that not only had I needed to eat but, if I wasn't sure how I was going to kill her yet, that she needed food also. I walked to the kitchen, over to the stove and cooked a large batch of eggs and bacon. After I ate my portion, I delivered the remaining breakfast to her.

Upon entering what I was now referring to as her room, I found her curled into a tight ball, fast asleep. I stepped inside, as quietly as possible in the attempt not to disturb her. As I placed the food beside her, she began to rouse and I took that as my cue to depart.

Chapter 6

The appetizing smell of bacon and eggs wafted throughout the room and I stirred from my restless slumber. I woke from a haze of dreams and looked around cautiously. He was nowhere to be seen, but just inches from my face lay a platter of warm food.

I fought my hunger momentarily as I examined it suspiciously. He hadn't killed me yet, but there was no reason why he couldn't poison the food. I sniffed it cautiously and my stomach rumbled. I hadn't eaten since yesterday morning before the fundraising event and I was starved. If I refused nourishment, I might as well have signed my life away and if the food was tainted, poison seemed more merciful than a knife.

Giving in; I picked up the fork, and shoveled in a big bite. Appreciating the taste, I gorged on the rest until the plate was clear. He had even thought to bring a glass of water, which I appreciated as I chugged the drink thirstily. Feeling settled from my meal, I got to my feet and strode over to the window. I had no way of telling what time it was, but I guessed it was early in the morning. It was a cloudy day and the sun only peeked out from behind the dark grey clouds occasionally. Would it rain or was it cold enough for snow?

As much as I hated to find anything positive about this experience, I admitted that the view was beautiful. I peered through the window with a sense of wonder. I had always enjoyed nature and this was no exception. The only thing keeping me sane had been my ability to focus on the view.

From what I could tell, we were far from the city and even if I managed to escape, I would probably have acres of woods to race through. I had a feeling that between his watchful eye on me and his dogs, my kidnapper would not let me get far. I also didn't want to anger him. He appeared very unstable and yesterday he hadn't, much to both of our surprises, killed me. I should have been dead by now; the way that man was possessed with evil. If there ever was anyone to spread the Devil's message, surely it was him. Yet I had no explanation for why I still lived. He had certainly proved that his killer ego was no bluff, but why had I been spared?

One of the really scary things was that he knew who I was. I wasn't just a random victim in the wrong place at the wrong time, he had planned this out. I know I had witnessed one of his crimes and that would make sense as to why he wanted me dead, but why had he put in all that time only to back away at the last moment? Besides, even if my status as a witness had influenced his feelings toward me; it didn't make sense as to why he would be afraid of me and telling his secrets. I didn't even know who he was. He had enough money and power to shield himself from anything. All I wanted to know was why and that is exactly what I asked him when he entered the room again a while later.

"Why?" he repeated in his gruff, masculine voice.

"Why go to all this trouble, instead of killing me even though that certainly seems like something you want to do."

He walked over and crouched beside me on the floor. "Originally, yes, I wanted to kill you—"

"But?"

"But now it would seem you are a dog," he said casually with the shrug of his shoulders. He was dressed casually today, with a plain T-shirt that showed off his powerful size. His hair was not perfectly groomed anymore, but flowed in loose blonde waves down to just above his eyes.

"Did you just call me a bitch?" I stumbled over the volatile word Arial used many times before. Normally, I didn't condone such language but I felt the need for something more powerful.

He looked at me for a moment as if he too found it weird to hear that come out of my mouth before he barked out a laugh, "Not in that way per se, but sure."

"What do you mean?" I asked for clarification.

He waved his hand and dismissed the thought, "That doesn't matter right now. I myself need some time to figure that out."

"Some time? Are you saying you are not going to kill me?" I asked. He shrugged his shoulders, "Another thing I need to figure out." "What am I really here for?"

"For me," he responded without missing a beat, "I'm a murderer. It's just part of who I am and I make no attempt to apologize for it. I kill people for fun and enjoy what their pain can give me. This will never change but there are certain limitations that I need to explore," he admitted before he lifted his head to look at me. As his cold blue gaze raked over mine I understood what he tried to convey. I was his weakness.

He paused to gather his words. "The only things I haven't been able to kill so far," he continued, "Are my dogs."

"You think I'm a dog?" I asked with a mix of offense. I didn't like being thought of as an animal, but I was relieved if it meant that I would remain alive for the time being.

He shrugged, "I don't know why I see you that way, that's

what I'm curious about."

"And how long do you plan to find this stuff out?" I asked nervously. "As long as it takes."

At that, I snapped. There was no way I was spending an immeasurable amount of time waiting for him to discover if he would kill me.

"I don't know what you think is going to happen, but if you let me go I promise nothing bad will come of it. I don't even know your name so there's no way I could get you into any trouble..." the idea crossed my mind. The only way I was going to get away from this place was if he released me. I didn't know where we were. Let alone who he really was so I had no tie here. I could make no claims against him and maybe if he too realized this; he would see nothing stopped him from letting me go.

He tilted his head in thought.

"There are some things we can never explain in life. Consider this one of those phenomena with no true explanation. You might never find the answers you seek and keeping me here forever would be a big burden, not to mention risky for you."

He narrowed his eyes and my heart rate increased excitedly. This was my only chance. It was risky, but it was all I had to offer.

I watched him contemplate my idea when I suddenly felt a horrible pressure against my neck. I gasped in air and looked down to find his hands wrapped tightly around my windpipe.

As quickly as the pressure had appeared, it disappeared.

"God dammit," he screamed at himself as he stood up. He walked over to the door and kicked it open angrily. He refused to look at me as he took a deep breath. "You get one chance," he hissed between his teeth, "NOW GET OUT!"

With that, I got up and charged out of the room, down the hallway, and finally outside. I didn't know which way to go or how far, but there was no way I was wasting this opportunity to escape. He could change his mind at any time, and I didn't want to be around when it happened.

52

Chapter 7

My hands trembled as I was struck with anger and confusion. *What did I just do?* For whatever reason, I'd allowed her to convince me to do something irrational. It was stupid, but she hit a nerve and I couldn't stand back and do nothing. Even though my decision was not well thought out, maybe it was for the best. She was right when she questioned my indecisiveness. I didn't know how long it would take to find whatever I searched for, and I did still have a life outside this strange obsession. As soon as the door slammed closed behind her and she receded into the line of trees, I was filled with a sense of regret. I wanted to chase after her, but forced myself to stay where I was. I knew she would not cause me any more trouble. Even if she tried to report me to authorities, which I doubted she had the backbone to do, I would easily get out of it. The only evidence was her word against my power.

I exhaled slowly and rested my forehead against the wall in an attempt to diffuse Cain. What was I hoping to accomplish with her anyway? I was curious why I struggled to hurt her, but even if I did find the answer. What would it do? Did I want to stop my murderous rampages? No, not really. At the thought of blood, my heart fluttered in anticipation. I knew the best way to get my mind off the situation, and it involved a lot of blood.

A quick look at the time reminded me that it was still early. It was easier to catch and finish victims under the cover of night, but I was so tightly wound that I needed to do something. I would just have to be really careful. I was already outside my normal dress, which always proved as good cover. I threw on my oversized black hoodie that completed my disguise, grabbed my keys, and headed to the garage. I almost forgot my treasured knife, and quickly turned around and snagged it before I left.

As I drove down the gravel path leading to my house, my thoughts kept wandering to her. How far had she gotten? Would she be alright? Would she wander back? I shook my head and cleared away those thoughts. There was no point wondering about it. I had made up my mind. She was on her own. Now I needed to enjoy what I was about to do.

I drove through the far outskirts of downtown. I knew better places, but if I got too busy in one spot; it would become too suspicious. I kept driving until I reached areas I had yet to explore. After I found a good spot, I parked a few blocks away from my intended destination. No matter how much I wanted to begin my slaughter, I followed all my cautionary steps regardless of how much time it required. Money and power had a limit. If I was caught in the middle of an attack. At that, my mind drifted back to Piper. *That was different!*

I strolled as casually as possible. It was hard not to get to where I wanted to go as fast as possible but if I rushed, it would raise suspicion.

I decided on a run-down connection of several alleyways filled with prostitutes and drug dealers. Like I had told the one person I couldn't kill, no one's life really matters to anyone else in the end, but that temporary moment before any attachment is severed; it sometimes was emotional. It would be easier to get rid of those who had no attachments. As an added bonus, the people who were caught up in those types of illegal activities were often assumed to be targeted by others in their field and one of their deaths would not be suspicious. No one would bat an eye at another dead drug addict. I passed by many potential victims, but none of them felt right. Too close to someone else, or too out in the open was not ideal.

Finally, I spotted her. All alone in a narrow alley, she immediately caught my attention. I walked into the secret crevice between the two abandoned buildings to where she sat. As I got closer, I finally got a good look at her. She didn't acknowledge me as she napped fitfully. She was incredibly lethargic with long blonde hair that fell in tangled grimy curls. She was dressed heavily in ragged clothing, but the small part of her arm that was exposed was covered in small needle sized bruises. The injection sites were an angry red and I scowled. How anyone could become so consumed in something that cost them so much was beyond me. I twirled the knife in my hand. At least Cain only hurt others, instead of me. I crouched down next to her and allowed the sharp blade of my knife to trace along the delicate contours of her youthful face. Her eyes twitched before she awoke with a start. She was about to jump up, but I shook my head and pressed a finger to my lips. It was then that she spotted the blade.

The confusion and terror was evident in her voice, "What do you want?" she rasped.

I pressed the blade against her mouth again and didn't hold back. A thin line of red appeared and began to spread.

"Please," she sobbed.

Normally I would have finished it, but today was different. After the very frustrating morning I had; I needed something a bit more memorable.

"Who are you?" I asked her.

"What?" she asked in an unsteady voice. Tears streamed down her face until they mixed with her blood as it spilled onto the blade that still pressed centimeters away from her mouth.

"Who are you?" I repeated.

She looked stunned at my question but quickly responded, "Bailey." I pressed the knife in harder as more thin flesh gave way. "No."

She cried harder now from pain and fear, "Yes I am—"

Before she finished her reply, I twisted the knife. She whimpered as I continued to dig into her mouth, "No. You are number five."

Her fear intrigued me and I laughed menacingly. I turned my hand so the sharp end of the blade pushed into her throat. With a flick, the point tore through the remaining tissue around her mouth until I felt the resistance of hardness. With a little added force, I managed to break through the layers of teeth until the blade reached the other side of her face. She tried to scream but it came out as a strangled sound as she choked on blood and other pieces of her crippled jaw. As she struggled, she coughed up a piece of her mangled tongue.

She was a miserable sight. Her face was helplessly marred by my knife. As amusing as it was, once her eyes started to roll back into her head, it was time to move on. She was losing consciousness and I needed to finish it. While I knew few people would approach this spot, I couldn't waste any more time. I pulled my arm back and dislodged my now bloodied knife from her maimed face. With practiced precision, I sliced through the weak veins and watched as the thin tubes of blood burst. Because of the unique angle, I had to move aside so that as the blood spurted, didn't get me drenched.

Since she was now unconscious, I never saw as her life faded like I had so many times before. I had turned away and left before all the blood could be spilled. This kill was different from the others. This one had been fueled by my inability to injure Piper. Since I hadn't been able to injure the one I really wanted to, I went overboard the moment I was able to inflict harm again. This was unlike me and I was worried that my unusual actions were a direct result of letting her go. Piper. Not only could I not kill her, but now she interrupted my methods of murder. It was so bad that I didn't even bother to watch the existence of my prey ebb away. She lay in the alley dying without me there to acknowledge her faded life.

As I headed back to my car, I spotted yet another possible victim. I turned my head to stop myself from doing it. My mood was sour and, as proven by the mutilated corpse in the alley, I was out of control. I tried to walk away, but the man who I considered as new prey ended walking in the same direction. There was no one else around that I could see and with him coming right toward me, there was little choice. I slowed down until his normal walking speed allowed him to catch up to me. He had headphones on and acknowledged me with a brisk nod. When he was about two feet in front of me, I withdrew my knife. I sped up and without hesitation, I reached my arm in front of him and skewered his neck with one clean slice.

I continued walking again at a normal pace without looking back. It was an incredibly reckless move, but I couldn't take it back. I just had to keep moving. I was lucky that the street was short and within a few long strides, I reached a corner.

Before I knew it, I was at my car. The path was relatively uneventful. I passed several other people along the way, but managed to get by without bringing any attention to myself.

Inside the car, I slammed my fists against the leather seats. What had I done? I was so out of control! Had I not been so lucky, I could have ruined everything I had worked for. Money, reputation, and power had been on the line, but I had been too focused on her. I was escalating and I needed some way to stop it. I sped off toward the only person whose presence I could tolerate. Stella.

****

I packed some spare clothes in my trunk. It made no sense in showing up while looking threatening. It was enough that I was dropping in unannounced and any other oddities would raise suspicion. Stella was very observant and there's no doubt she would already sense something was off, but I didn't need to contribute to that with a scraggly appearance.

When I was certain I looked fine with no remnants of blood, I walked up to the front door of her small house. It was located in a small but quaint neighborhood, which was a far cry away from my lonely estate.

As I waited for Stella to answer the door, I noticed the painted paneling along the sides of her house had faded and peeled. Against my instincts, I made a mental note to not mention it. My sister was very defensive about her humble abode and didn't appreciate me combing through its minor flaws. It was a small one-story home with two bedrooms and one bathroom. While I had offered her money for a larger dwelling, she refused and said she would earn it herself. I hadn't touched the subject any further and she always seemed proud of her modest house whenever I came to visit. *How nice it must be to find fulfillment from such simple things.*

I knocked again and tapped my foot in a quick staccato by the time she finally answered. Upon noticing her, I laughed outright with the first ounce of honest humor I had had in a while. She was dressed in a pink pair of cotton pajamas that did little to attest to her maturity.

"Sylas!" she exclaimed. She frowned when she heard my laughter. She looked down at her outfit, "What? It's early!"

I shook my head, "It's almost noon, sis," I corrected.

She slapped me on the shoulder, "That's early to me! I was still sleeping, dumbass–oh whatever," She moved to the side and motioned for me to come in with a wave of her hand. "To what do I owe this wonderful pleasure," she drawled sarcastically as she did a bow. She scrunched her eyebrows. "Aren't you supposed to be on vacation?" she questioned.

"Flight was cancelled," I mumbled as I strode through the small space used as a living room and plopped down on the couch.

"Well, that's a bummer," She raked a hand through her disheveled shoulder length blonde hair.

Despite the four years that separated us–Stella, 23 and I, 27–our shockingly similar bright blonde hair and ice blue eyes made it possible for us to pass as twins. Stella's tall, lanky figure and my own muscular one with sharp features had been known to turn heads.

"Yeah, it's fine though, there will always be plenty of time for someone like me to go on vacation. Maybe next time I'll just buy the island. That'll be faster!" A pillow flew from her arms and slammed me in the face. Although I was naturally very serious in nature, years of jokes and banter throughout my childhood allowed me to interact normally with my only sibling.

As I watched her make herself a bowl of cereal, I wondered if she was anything like Piper. While my sister was one of the select few alive whom I could tolerate and didn't necessarily want dead, I wondered if I could kill her. It would have been such an inconvenience if I lost my only social outlet, and a part of me knew I did have the capacity to do such a thing. It didn't mean I would kill her as there were so many other targets with whom I had no connection to and that I would easily kill when the urge struck, but it didn't mean that I couldn't do it. As much as I valued our sibling camaraderie, I knew there was a chance I would feel little to no remorse if I sliced her neck wide open.

"You hungry?" Stella asked with a mouthful of cereal.

"No thanks," I declined and joked, "Some of us have already

ate lunch." She rolled her eyes and took another bite, "I'm a late sleeper," she protested.

When she finished her so-called breakfast, she sat down in the plush chair opposite the couch.

"So, I get that your trip was cancelled and all, Mr. Rich Boy, but why exactly are you here? I mean, not that I mind or anything but you're usually so methodical about visiting. I'm surprised you didn't call in advance."

"Do I need a reason?" I retorted and motioned toward her to remind her of all her impromptu visits.

She lifted her hand in surrender, "Okay, fine I get it. But it's still a two- hour drive and you tend to prefer auditory communication over in person."

I sighed loudly, "I just needed a little change, that's all," I admitted.

She nodded, "I feel you. While I'm glad that the guy who killed dad finally got what was coming to him it still brings up a lot of emotions," her eyes misted over slightly but I could tell from the stubborn pout in her jaw that she refused to let any tears fall.

"Yeah," I agreed. I was glad there was an excuse to blame my visit on since I didn't know how to explain what was going through my mind. At the same time though, I didn't want to upset Stella further. I was bad at handling my own emotions, let alone other people's. I didn't know how to react when someone was upset, and Stella was no exception. "Anyway," I began to change the topic, "I do have something that I could use your insight on."

She perked up immediately. She was one of those people who did not waste an opportunity if someone wanted to hear their opinion, "Ok, shoot."

"Well you know how I have my dogs," I started and paused until she nodded for me to continue, "I don't really know how to describe it but I found something that's not a dog but reminds me of one," I stumbled over the best way to phrase it and in the end cursed how incompetent I sounded.

"It's called a cat, Sy," she remarked sassily.

I dragged my hand down my face in an exaggerated manner. "That's not what I'm talking about," She giggled in a juvenile manner and it was hard to see a full-grown woman instead of a young kid across from me. I hiked up an eyebrow until she quieted, "I can't really describe what it is, but something about it is so reminiscent of my dogs… but it's certainly not canine."

"Does it bark?" "No."

"Will it fetch?" "Stella," I grumbled.

"Well, then why do you think it's like a dog? I'm gonna

need you to elaborate here, bro, because I have no idea what's going on. Are you sure you're not just finally seeing how great cats can be?"

"I still hate cats," I clarified. "But I don't know what it is. It's certainly not a physical characteristic but when I see her all I can think of are my dogs, but not in a bad way!"

At Stella's intake of breath, I realized I had accidentally slipped a pronoun in, "Oh, I would say invite me to the wedding but I don't think she will appreciate being called a dog!"

I groaned, "Stella, seriously."

She did her best to hide the excitement and curiosity that had annoyed me, but I still saw it sparkled in her eyes. She paused a moment to think and then added, "We're going to talk about this later, but for right now I'll help. I am very confused though. Anyway, you said it was not a physical characteristic so she's not furry and doesn't slobber–thank God!" she grinned when she saw my agitated expression. "So that just leaves the 'man's best friend' characteristics. Hmm, is she loyal? Playful? Sweet? Innocent?"

I didn't hear anything past that. My mind was spinning as I suddenly connected the dots. I might not have known much about her, but one thing was glaringly obvious. She was different from everyone else with her purity. Those things she said about people's lives mattering, along with her association with her church and other charities made it clear as to why I couldn't take her life. The whole reason I felt no remorse when I killed was because I hated humans. But I had only classified humans as selfish, manipulative beings. While that applied to almost everyone past a certain age; there was a lack of awareness in her trusting nature. She had yet to be tainted. She was a puppy in my world. Innocent and above the ways of everyone else. It was no wonder when I looked into her brown eyes, all I could see was a dog. She reminded me of how I had found Daisy as I pup. I remembered the scrawny black and white puppy that had limped up to my house coated in dirt with thin, matted fur. Rather than put the poor dog out of its misery, I took it in and fought on its behalf, until it was a healthy dog whose only devotion was to me.

She wasn't a dog, though, which meant she wouldn't always remain sweet and trusting. I had found my answer. If I wanted to kill her and get rid of this complication, which continued to plague me, then I would need to remove that part of her that made her so different from everyone else. She was the one who said I corrupted others. Now was the time to try it out.

I changed the subject of our discussion quickly after that and chatted idly with my sister. She talked about her life, along with all its insignificant details that I absorbed, but didn't really care for.

I made a big gesture out of checking the time on my phone, "Well, it was great catching up, Stell, but it's getting late and I still have to drive back."

She had since gotten dressed and put makeup on in the time I had been there and no longer donned those funny pajamas, though her initial appearance would definitely make a humorous story for later. "Alright, talk to you later," Before I could leave she added, "Oh! And if you see any new information on that Gravo case, let me know!"

"You do realize that I'm not a police officer, right?"

She sighed dramatically and said, "I mean if you see anything on the news, be sure to tell me. I'm very interested to see if they can find out who caused it."

I had to refrain from releasing the ironic laugh that bubbled in my throat, "I don't usually watch the news, but if I see anything I'll be sure to contact you," Her satisfactory nod was my parting cue and I exited the small house and eased into my car along the side of the road. The driveway hadn't been big enough for both our cars, but I trusted the small neighborhood enough to park along the curb.

It was a tedious drive back to my own home; as there was no one immediate path. After I navigated through a bunch of bumpy backroads, it was a relief to accelerate along the smooth interstate. I was rushing home to further formulate my plan. I understood it was highly unlikely that she was still on the property. There was one main patch where the trees went on for acres, but it was only in a single direction. All she had to do was follow the driveway or go in one of the other directions and it would only take a bit of walking. It still wouldn't be a quick escape. Certainly, she was smart enough to figure that out because with the dropping temperatures, it would be miserable.

Knowing that she was probably far away now, I would have to review the information I had gathered on her. Maybe it was cheap to go back on my original decision to let her escape but in the end, she still knew too much about me. Even if she never used any of that knowledge, the fact that she had been a nuisance that tempered with my already small amount of control was enough to feel my vengeance. In the end, despite the way she managed to suppress Cain, was less impressive than the way I would feel staring upon her body.

The thought of her death bothered me deeply. I knew I needed to act quickly, in order to taint her image before I lost the opportunity completely. The moment I no longer carried a bizarre torch for her, she would be mine to kill.

Chapter 8

The cold wind whipped my hair around and I shivered into the long cotton tee that was my only source of heat. I rubbed my hands together frantically to create the friction that prevented my fingers from becoming numb. I wasn't dressed for the frigid temperatures that had dropped overnight. Yesterday had been unseasonably warm and the outfit I had worn to the fundraising event had been much more appropriate. Now, however, it left me exposed. Wracked with shivers, I was shaky as I headed down the narrow back street.

The moment I escaped from his clutches, I had run straight to the driveway. It was the only way I could think, to get away from him without getting lost. *Christ! Did he have enough money to buy a whole forest? What is up with all these trees?* The path led to a connecting road as predicted, but it was still a much longer walk than I imagined. Of course, he would have his slaughterhouse hidden deep in the wilderness away from curious eyes.

I reached the road at last after a long jog through what I now referred to as The Jungle. If it had been a real jungle, though, I would have welcomed the humidity. My lungs rasped the chilly air and my throat burned at the exertion. To make matters worse, the clouds had darkened and the sun was nowhere to be seen. It was hard enough to trudge along as it was, I didn't need snow to make it any more difficult. The road was already pretty empty and if it got icy, the minimal flow of traffic would become nonexistent. I had never hitchhiked before, but I assumed I had the thumb gesture down correctly.

Eventually, when I risked turning into an ice cube in the arctic weather, a car slowed down. An older, black Honda model eased to a stop on the side of the road, just a couple feet away from me. The front window opposite the driver's seat rolled down and I was greeted by an elderly woman. She pushed her thin glasses up her nose and asked if I needed a ride. I nodded nervously, my throat too raw to respond. Upon hearing the door unlock, I climbed inside.

"Thank you," I sputtered through chattered teeth. Other than asking for directions as to where I needed to go, the ride was relatively silent. By the time we reached my destination, the car's heater had done its job and I was defrosted.

"Thank you again, I really appreciate your generosity," I thanked the older woman.

She dismissed me with a wave of her hand, "You looked like you needed some help. I don't usually pick up strangers, but you looked harmless and the way you were shivering—" she drifted off at the end and with a sweet smile, pulled away.

I looked around the neighborhood I had grown familiar with in all my visits. I noted the police car parked nearby. I wasn't surprised since some of Arial's neighbors were known to throw rather boisterous parties, which left them acquainted with members of the force.

Before I even knocked on the door, it swung open and I was greeted by Arial.

"Oh, my God!" she exclaimed with relief.

"Hey," I said meekly as she welcomed me inside.

"Where the hell were you?" she demanded.

I winced. "Language," I corrected. She rolled her eyes at my censorship. "It's a long story," I answered as I stumbled into the kitchen.

"Um," Arial warned too late.

Seated at the round kitchen table were two police officers. One was a burly woman who looked anything but pleased to be there, and the other was a young man who look around a rookie's eagerness.

"Are you, by any chance, Piper Rowan?" the large woman asked.

I nodded my head in confusion, "Yes, Ma'am," I answered.

The younger one's eyes looked up in curiosity. It took me a moment to realize what he stared at as I cupped my damaged cheek with my right hand. The cold had a numbing effect and I had almost completely forgotten about the small wound. The Band-Aid was still in place, but some of the blood had continued to seep through and there was a red stain across its bandage.

The other woman stared at my face with scrutiny. Her eyes stopped where my hand touched my cheek, but then quickly moved on in disinterest.

"We have some questions for you," the man piped in.

"Questions?"

I looked to Arial from her position as she leaned against the wall. Her fingers combed through her hair nervously. "When I couldn't find you yesterday, I tried to locate your phone and when it showed nothing, I knew something was up. After you didn't come home yesterday either, I assumed something had happened and I contacted the police." She took in her bright outfight that contrasted with Arial's dark skin.

"She was trying to file a missing person's report," the large officer said in a deep voice as her hand rested along her second chin, "But then your name showed the location of your apartment."

I struggled to find the significance of my apartment when my mind flashed back to the first time I had looked into those icy eyes that had now haunted more than just my dreams. The murder that had taken place must have made my dwelling a red flag.

Even though I understood my locations importance, I asked, "What does that have to do with anything?"

The woman scowled. Her glare told me she didn't believe my question. She knew that I understood the connection, "We need to take your statement," she ordered.

"But why, I know nothing about what happened," I replied and it took all my control to keep my voice from trembling. I had never really lied before, but I hoped I was convincing.

"Anything you can tell us will be helpful. Did you know Charles Gravo well?" the younger cop added.

"He was a nice man but I don't know much beyond that—"

"But you did know him," the woman stated. There was no question in her voice.

"Yeah, I guess," It was already difficult enough to omit any information

I knew about the killer, so I chose to be as truthful as I could.

"So, the reports of you helping him from time to time are truthful?"

"I mean, I would occasionally help him with groceries and stuff," I admitted, "He was nice, but his age made it a bit difficult for him to do everything. I was merely being a good neighbor."

The two officers exchanged a glance, and I could have sworn the woman had a look of triumph. "You wouldn't mind coming down to the station then," she asked, "If you want to help us bring justice for this poor man, then even the smallest bit of your time could be crucial in solving the case."

I must have already looked a mess and refusing to go after saying how I was friendly toward him, would make me appear suspicious. I hadn't done anything wrong so I had nothing to worry about. I could repent for my lies later, but I'd hate to impede an investigation. Besides, if my information could help them find the killer then many future lives would be saved. I had promised I wouldn't lead them back to him, but if they arrived at their own conclusions then it couldn't be traced back to me. "Okay," I agreed.

Arial looked at me in shock and I hoped that she understood my mental promise to explain things later.

It was awkward riding in the police car to the station but once we arrived, as promised, things moved very quickly. Within the span of about an hour I told them as much as I could, but excluded all the parts of what I had witnessed. After it was over, I was promised a ride back to Arial's house. When I was waiting for my chauffeurs to return, I overheard a hushed conversation in one of the breakrooms by the bathroom. The unmistakable deep voice of the large woman who had questioned me at Arial's home was audible.

"I just don't get it. It doesn't add up. We have no solid evidence against whoever killed the guy."

"What did the neighbor tell you about him," an unfamiliar voice asked thoughtfully.

"Nothing important. That girl is squeaky clean. Did you know apparently its considered neighborly to help carry in someone else's groceries?"

Although I knew she was making fun of me, I recognized there was more to what they said.

The other person's voice dropped to a hushed tone "Wait a minute, did you say that she helped with the groceries."

"I know, right? I gotta get myself some of them over gracious neighbors."

"No, you're missing the point!" the other person demanded. "What are you talking about?"

"Weren't there spilled groceries at the scene of the crime?"

Everything went silent and I felt sick. My stomach turned at their implication. I needed to get away before matters got worse.

I walked away and went to the front of the station where the male cop from earlier offered to take me home. I needed to leave the station quickly, and I made a show of how urgently I needed to return. The officer understood my concern and politely obliged. He went ahead and dropped me off even without his partner present.

"You have a good day now," he said politely.

"I hope I've helped," I said as we parted. I only hoped that my 'help' didn't amount to my own arrest.

Arial was waiting in the living room when I returned, "What was that about? What happened? Where were you yesterday?" I stuck a hand up to stop the slew of questions. There was only so many I could answer at a time.

"I'm so sorry about yesterday!" I apologized knowing how concerned she must have been.

"What happened?"

I racked my brain for the best excuse. "Well, um, after

the event someone had offered to buy some drinks and I had never done something like that before. I didn't want to be left out so I said I would go. Unfortunately, I have zero tolerance for alcohol and next thing I knew it was morning. I didn't have my phone and woke with a cut on my face," it went against my moral code to even suggest something as irresponsible as drinking alcoholic beverages, but I figured it was the only reference Arial would really understand.

She looked at me incredulously, "Are you telling me that you, goody- two-shoes Piper, got drunk?"

After my nervous nod, she burst into a fit of laughter, "Oh my God I wish I could have seen that, ha-ha and then you passed out!" she laughed so hard; she sputtered her last few words.

"It was a mistake," I rubbed my temples.

"A mistake I would have PAID to see!" when she finally calmed down and stopped her fit of giggles, she added, "But what were those cops saying about that other dude?"

"About a week ago, the old man who lived above me was found dead. They just wanted my opinion to see if he could have had any enemies or someone that would do such a thing."

She was silenced at that and had the decency to remain stoic. In her most serious voice she asked, "Is that the reason you came to stay here?"

I nodded. "I'd been wanting to move out and when I realized just how close someone I knew was killed, I had to get out."

"Well, that makes a lot of sense, but why didn't you tell me in the first place?"

I shrugged casually.

She narrowed her eyes suspiciously.

"What?"

"You're the most honest person I know. Why did you refuse to talk about something like that? You know I would've helped you."

"I was just stunned, that's all—"

She gave me one last look before she let the subject go. She wasn't going to push it any further, but her curiosity meant she would eventually bring it up again. "Well, I'm gonna make some grilled cheese for lunch. Would you, by any chance, want some?"

I smiled contently. She was offering to make my favorite food, and she knew I wouldn't resist.

Lunch was peaceful as I listened to some more of Arial's usual gossip while I savored my cheesy sandwich. Although it was a delightful meal, I was occupied with other thoughts. What I had heard the cops said, distressed me the most. I had a nagging feeling that it wouldn't be the last I heard from them. I would have to be careful. While I was a law-abiding citizen, who followed the rules word for word, my involvement could be considered strange. I knew that the real killer was a very smart man and I knew there would not be enough, if any, clues left behind to incriminate him. Unfortunately, that left me as the only viable suspect if they reached that point of thought.

While I hated lying and going against authority, I knew this was different. *Should I choose to follow my righteous path and admit what I know?* Even if it will lead to them thinking I was responsible and facing time for something I didn't do. Should I hope I have enough good karma to get out of it *or* run away, and hope that by some odd means they find the real killer. All of that deep thinking was quickly led to a headache and I excused myself after I had finished eating and went to lie down on the bed in the guest room I had occupied.

Whenever I tried to close my eyes though, I was flooded with images of him. I wasn't afraid. If anything, the thought of him filled me with intrigue. As much as I hated him and despised his evil actions, he was unique. I had so many questions for him. I guess he wasn't the only curious one. I wanted to know what fueled his devilish mind and what caused him to be the way he was. I worked part-time as a nurse's assistant, but I had always been interested in psychology.

Was it possible that he had some disorder, or was he just the product of something much more sinister?

Chapter 9

It had been nearly two days since I allowed *her* to escape and those 48 hours had been some of the most maddening of my life. I had made a big mistake letting her walk free, but I was going to make up for it in due time.

As I pulled the gag into place, I looked closely at the dilated brown eyes staring up at me. Restrained to a chair, the muscular man sized me up in a meager attempt to appear tough. He was nervous though, as evident by the sheen of sweat covering his dark skin. I checked the chains wrapped around his arms and torso one last time to assure that they were inescapable. Satisfied that he would not be making an appearance sooner than necessary, I walked out of the room and locked the door. It was so hard to walk away from him when he was so helpless. It would be so easy to slice his throat in that position, but he was not mine to kill. He would not be my victim, but a way to lure out someone else's darkness.

I heard the rattle of chains and the thumping of chair legs. It was muted slightly due to the plush carpet, but the unmistakable sound of a crash still reverberated through the house. I smirked. The fool must have tried to squirm free and knocked the chair over in his attempt. I hoped he was comfortable on his side then because I was not going to go help him. Now that I had a live audience, though, I began the next part of my plan.

I was almost giddy with excitement as I typed the address I had acquired into my GPS. This should lead me to the residence of an Arial Mitchel. I pushed the speed limit as I drove, unable to wait any longer. It had already taken me enough time to get this together and I needed to get a move on.

I didn't waste any time getting out of my car and knocking on the door as soon as I pulled up to where *she* was.

The person who answered the door, however, was not the female I had hoped for. A tall, enthusiastic woman came to my summons instead. With styled, black hair that flowed to the edge of a skimpy outfit, I assumed that the woman must have been Arial. Her dark eyes darted up and down as she took me in with a sweeping glance.

She stuck a manicured hand out which I shook, "How can I help you?" she asked with a rasp.

Part of me had wondered if Piper's friends would be anything like her in the sense that I wouldn't be able to kill them because of her innocent nature. I was wrong. I would slice this one's throat in a heartbeat.

"Ah, I'm here for Piper," I spoke with a beaming smile. I had to be on my best behavior to pull this off.

She welcomed me inside without any further questions. "I don't think she's ever mentioned you," she motioned toward me with her hand.

"It's Sylas."

"I don't think she's ever mentioned you before, Sylas, but then again she's not big on talking about personal stuff."

"Indeed," I agreed, "So, where is she? She said she was staying here."

"Oh yeah. She is staying here, but she went to go visit her parents today. It's a bit of a drive, unfortunately, but she should be back either late tonight or tomorrow."

"She went to her parent's house?"

"Yeah, it was kind of random, but she said she hadn't seen them in a while and she wanted to check in," her words seemed honest and I trusted what she said.

"So, she's not here," I confirmed. "I'm afraid not," she apologized.

"Well alright then, it was nice meeting you," I offered as I started to turn away. Before I could finish, though, the sound of police sirens, which had been distant at first, suddenly amplified until I could see the blue and white flashing from the front window.

"What the—" I spoke as two officers rushed out of the vehicle and toward the house. I looked at Arial and wondered if Piper had given a description of me. My chest tightened at the thought of betrayal, and I was taken over with anger until the shocked look on Arial's face showed that she hadn't expected this either.

She rushed forward and opened the door the policemen had been knocking on. They stormed inside and one of them announced, "I have the warrant for the arrest of Piper Rowan."

What happened?

"What?" Arial screeched, "What is this about?"

The man shoved past her and looked at me, "We were told that she had been staying at this residence and she was present the last time we were here. Where is she?"

"She left," I answered on cue, "She was only staying here a few nights. Now she's back at her grandmother's."

"Her grandmother's house?" He hiked up a brow in question.

"Yes," Arial responded in corroboration. "But I don't know

the exact location, I'm afraid."

Not convinced, they performed a quick sweep of the house. When they returned one of the men grunted to the other, "Guess we have to locate this other property she is staying." He looked to us, "But if you hear anything else, you guys be sure to let us know. This is not a case that can be taken lightly, even if she is your friend."

When they had left, I turned to Arial, "What was that about?"

She shook her head loosely, "I don't know! They came to ask some questions about the incident that happened in her apartment building."

"The murder," I said when it looked like she wasn't going to say it.

She looked at me, her green eyes wide, "You don't think—no—there's no way!"

"There's definitely no way it's true," I confirmed. "But, even if it's not, we need to find her now."

She nodded in agreement.

"Do you know where her parents' house is?"

"Yeah! She gave me the address a while ago. Hold on—" she dashed and began frantically shuffling through various drawers, until she found the small piece of paper where the address was written. Omitting the fact that I already knew the location, I let Piper's friend ramble. I could have done it by myself, but I had a feeling it would be useful to bring Arial along. I couldn't just waltz up to the house, and she would serve as a great lure. Of course, I could always kill her parents but that would be too hard with multiple targets so I would have to settle for bringing the friend along.

"We'll take my car," I told her as I ushered her out of the house and toward my expensive vehicle.

I was worried she would protest, but one look at my car and she was sold. It was certainly an upgrade from the orange Jeep in the driveway. I turned the heat up as she plugged the directions into the GPS. The temperature had continued to drop to the point where it was impossible to argue that it was anything besides winter. Arial didn't seem affected by the weather, or at least that's what her choice of clothing indicated. Even though I was comfortable in my tailored suit, I figured she would appreciate the extra warmth.

Partway into the drive Arial tried to strike a conversation, "So, what do you think happened?"

"With Piper?"

"Yeah."

"Well, we both know she wasn't involved with the

crime, but that doesn't mean that wrongful conclusions can't hurt her," I paused. The scenery flashed in the periphery as the car accelerated, "I'll figure it out," I gritted my teeth.

"What do you mean?" her question was innocent, but it still managed to grate my nerves.

"Trust me, I will figure it out," I snapped back a little more angrily than I meant to.

This was quickly becoming a horrible complication. I had been sure not to leave anything at the scene of the crime and had covered for her when I removed the items she touched. I hadn't thought about the fact that she had helped him before I arrived. Who knew what type of damning clues she had left. Her prints would have been everywhere. My grip tightened on the steering wheel until my knuckles were white. Arial flinched a bit at my retort and unbridled annoyance, but she was smart to make no further comment.

If the police got to Piper before I could, there would be nothing I could do. She was mine. I had yet to further explore what was so special about her, and I still planned to kill her. If I didn't eventually get a chance to finish things, though, I would be haunted by her sweet gaze forever. At least, if I was able to look into those eyes as she died, I would be able to expel those strange feelings that cluttered my mind. Such a scenario, however, would be inconceivable if she fell into the possession of the law. A tick worked its way along my jaw as I considered the possibility of failure. I couldn't afford to lose the game I'd begun. If that meant recapturing Piper to fulfill my agenda before any evidence could be pinned against her, then I needed to work fast.

After another half hour passed, Arial regained her confidence and tried to talk to me again, "So, how did you meet Piper."

"Church event," I answered curtly.

"Cool," She closed her mouth as she thought of what to say next, "Do you have any pets?"

It was a random question until I noticed my phone flashed with a

message. She must have seen the outline of one of the dogs on my lock screen. "I have four dogs."

"Oh, wow!" her enthusiasm had returned as she found a good topic to talk about, "What breeds?"

As it was one of the few things I didn't mind discussing, I responded, "They are all mutts."

"Rescued?" she asked as she grabbed my bicep. At my nod, she added, "Aw, that's sweet! What are their names?"

I looked at her out of the corner of my eye, until she released my arm. Reigning in my distaste for the woman in the seat beside mine, I focused on the few beings whose existence I didn't find atrocious. "Simon's mainly Shepherd, but he's got a bright white coat. Rebel is the biggest of the group and he's predominantly Rottweiler, but because of his size I suspect a bit of Mastiff as well. Buster is a fluffy, but lazy excuse for a Chow, and Daisy is my herding mix," I hoped I included enough details to ignore any follow-up questions. I didn't mind talking about my dogs, but it felt too personal to fully discuss with a stranger.

"I bet Piper loves them," she exclaimed with a wink, "She loves everyone and everything!"

Everyone except for me that is. I wanted to correct her, but kept the humorous irony to myself.

Getting comfortable, Arial started talking about herself. She became so absorbed in making sure she told me every detail; she was telling me about her other friends that she failed to notice I wasn't listening. At least she stopped expecting me to respond.

After another hour or so, our little road trip came to an end as I made one final turn onto the street where the house was located.

I opened my door and climbed out as Arial followed suit. "What's the plan?" she asked.

I didn't answer her and went straight ahead and rang the doorbell.

A man, well into his sixties, opened the door. A crop of silvery hair covered his head, but there was a darker pigment sprinkled throughout that revealed the once dark hue. His dark brown eyes and thin nose confirmed that we were in the right place. His daughter definitely resembled him.

"You must be Mr. Rowan," I greeted.

He nodded slowly. His face was solemn and the lines around his mouth were proof that his strict expression was not a temporary one.

"I've brought my friend Arial along with me," I said and he nodded in recognition at Arial, "I'm sorry to bother you, but Piper happened to leave something important behind and we've come here to deliver it," He gave me a stern look and I added, "If I could just borrow her for a moment."

"Fine," he said gruffly before returning to the other side of the door, "Piper!" he called.

I heard the second set of footsteps approaching, and then the next face that popped out from behind the front door was Piper's. Her father had receded into the house with a huff. Piper's eyes scanned the area curiously.

She noticed Arial first and instantly greeted her loyal friend. While she was locked in Arial's embrace, her eyes met mine and widened in horror. It would appear she had not forgotten my face this time. I could tell she was about to scream, so I placed one finger over my lips and slid another across my throat.

She understood the gesture and remained quiet. She stepped away from Arial and began to inch back inside the house. I grabbed her arm and pulled her close, "Piper!" I exclaimed with enough enthusiasm to fool Arial, "So good to see you. Now, come here, I have something to show you—"

She was reluctant, but I managed to drag her toward the car. She kept glancing at Arial in confusion. When we reached the vehicle, I pulled her into my arms for a hug of my own. She remained rigid as I leaned my head over and whispered in her ear, "I know where all of them live. You will get in the car or I will pull out my knife and make more than just Arial's hair red. If you don't cooperate, we'll see how well that little mermaid swims in her own blood."

She swallowed loudly, "You wouldn't," she stammered. "Try me," I enticed as I pulled away from her face.

Arial came to stand next to us, "We're here to help!"

Piper looked between both of us crazily, "What?" she asked. I shrugged, "Long story," I remarked casually.

"Yup," Arial agreed. She elbowed Piper and added, "But you sure are lucky Sylas is here to help."

Her chocolate eyes flicked to me as she took in the information. She still hadn't heard my name up until this point, and now she certainly understood what it meant. When I had released her before; it was because I knew she had no ties to me, but with my name now in her vocabulary, she was stuck. That final tether had been put in place, and it meant that I was not letting her go. The only escape would be death.

"Arial, do you mind if the two of us talk for a moment?"

"No!" Piper responded first. I stared at her menacingly until she caved under the weight of my unspoken threat, "Ok."

Arial gave us a weird look then started to head toward the house, "I have to go to the bathroom so I'll leave you two to talk," she turned around and trotted up to the house. She opened the door and walked in as if she was familiar with the place. The second she vanished from view, the real confrontation began. "What are you doing here?" she hissed at me, "I haven't done anything!

You are safe. You horrible, sadistic man!"

"It's not what I've done this time though," I barked. *Okay, technically it is, but I don't need to admit that!* "I'm not the one being arrested for murder."

Shock registered across her face first. After a brief pause her surprise was followed by understanding.

I walked around the side of the car and threw the door ajar. "Now, get in," I commanded.

"I don't have to!" she mouthed back, "I could just call the authorities right now and have my name cleared!"

"And how long would that take? Long enough for me to get away, I think. Plus, it's useless. I have allies on the force and too much money to ever be touched. No one will pay your delusions any mind." In actuality, I had no connections to any officers. Taking away any shred of optimism, I'd found, was a useful tactic. The last part was a lie, but it did its job. Her resolve shattered, but she was still determined. "Now get in or I come back whenever the time arises and destroy those people you claim to care for," I threatened with the click of my tongue. I gestured toward the house.

Her deepening frown indicated my victory. She was so intriguingly selfless that she wouldn't even risk the lives of others if she could stop it herself. It was foolish and in the long run would get her killed, but it sure was convenient for me.

As she sat down inside the vehicle, I commented, "Much comfier than the trunk, huh?"

She didn't appreciate my comment, "They'll be worried," she spoke softly and I knew she referred to her parents and Arial.

"Emotions are annoying, but they are a sign of living," I offered.

It was another gesture she didn't appreciate, "I could easily lean over and turn the steering wheel. It would take too long for you to correct it." Her threat hung in the air, and I was surprised with the amount of malice her words carried.

"You wouldn't do that. Too risky."

"What makes you think I wouldn't?" She seemed almost offended that I had assumed the best in her.

I kept my eyes on the road and refused to let her feel as if her words had any impact. "Because as much as you might hate me, you wouldn't risk it. The chance for injury to both of us is high and, despite the fact that you want to stop me, you wouldn't actually hurt me. You admitted yourself that while you did not wish me the best, justice was something you didn't have the right to inflict. Someone so strong in her beliefs wouldn't fold so easily," while it might make it harder to get home, part of me wanted her to act that way. If her threats extended beyond idle, maybe then I would stop viewing her as some innocent puppy. Maybe then, I would see her as a human. Maybe, I would finally see her as prey. But, as I

73

predicted, she did nothing.

She was shocked into silence for a moment. I was no contractor, but I had hit the nail on the head. "I don't hate you," she mumbled at last. I glanced suspiciously in her direction. "Because," she elaborated, "Hate is a powerful emotion. With your cruelty, you deserve no emotion whatsoever. "

"You think I really care what you think about me?"

"Yes," she responded firmly. "You thrive off power. I see it in the way you talk about your victims. You feed from their fear, and it empowers you."

I clenched my teeth together and a tick worked its way around my jaw as her words hit close to home, "So, what are you going to do? Deny your own fear?"

"No, but I'm going to deny my hate. You are just a bully, and I'm going to refuse to feed your ego."

Her statement of indifference, despite my stoic appearance, really bothered me in a way I couldn't explain. I convinced myself it shouldn't matter though. When the moment came, not even she would be able to cut off her emotions with a knife perched at her neck. My thoughts wandered back to the man tied up in my house. She made bold claims and even if she tried to make them true, I would find a way to break her. And then I would finally get what I waited for.

It was a slow drive all the way back and I was lucky that I didn't need to stop along the way. My car would be in desperate need of gas by the time I returned to my estate, but it was better than risking, making any stops.

Piper remained silent in her seat, but her eyes never left me. She was watching my every move. She was smart not to trust me, but what she didn't realize was that I still had some work to do before I could even indulge in some gore.

When I pulled into the driveway and parked in the garage, I half expected her to leap out and try to escape but she remained still. I reached over the seat and grabbed her head. She struggled until I had my full arm wrapped around her neck. I held her in that position until her head lolled back and I released her unconscious form. She looked peaceful with her eyes closed and had I not just partially strangled her, I would have assumed she was asleep.

My hands were shaking as I carried her inside the house. It had taken all my willpower to even do something as simple as knock her unconscious. I still had a lot of work to do if I hoped to change her.

I brought her into the room she had stayed in previously. The man tied to the chair struggled and whimpered when he noticed me, but he uselessly flailed in his overturned seat. It was comical and pathetic all at the same time.

I placed Piper gently in the corner. My fingers lingered momentarily on the soft material of her light blue blouse. Instead of leaving her to wake up on her own, I took a seat next to her and pulled her into my chest. For whatever reason, I felt the need to be there when she woke. The entire time I held her, I maintained eye contact with my other hostage. As Piper began to rouse, I placed her back on the carpet and walked out of the room. I needed to grab my prized knife in order to make things more interesting.

When I returned, she had sat up and looked around the room while she rubbed her eyes, "What?" she asked groggily as she looked at the man spilled on the ground in front of her.

"Do you like it?" I asked with a devilish grin, "I brought some target practice."

"What the heck is wrong with you?" she screeched.

I shrugged and revealed the knife I held. I looked at the man sprawled on the floor. I gasped dramatically, "My goodness, you are right!" I said in an unnaturally playful manner. I reached down and grabbed the gag from his mouth and continued my act. "Phew, that's much better," I sarcastically drawled.

I wasn't usually so playful with my victims, but I was in a good mood. Tonight, I would hopefully not have just one victim, but two. Maybe I would finally be able to silence that nagging voice that told me to stop. *Cain will free me from my suffering.*

I righted the man's chair so that he was once again in an upright position. The moment I did so, he screamed hysterically. It was loud and I cupped my ears. When he stopped to take a deep breath, I said, "The gag was for my own safety. You are on my property and no one will hear you."

He was breathing heavily, "I will kill you," he seethed.

"I'm afraid that's usually my job," I corrected. I leaned in close and, with my face inches from his, whispered, "Maybe you'll get a second chance in Hell, though." I pulled away and walked over to the door and locked it.

I turned to the victim whom I found more concerning. "Piper," I said smoothly, "I might have found a way for you to keep your family safe—"

She eyed the knife and instantly understood the implications, "No."

"No?" I asked. When she shook her head disobediently, I moved back to my other prey. Without even the slightest hesitation I slashed wildly with the blade. The man screamed pathetically, and I scowled. The cut along his forehead was relatively shallow, and he'd forfeited any farce of heroism with that pitiful wail. I wanted to hit somewhere more vital, but I restrained myself from drawing too much blood. His spirit wasn't mine to take. Today, it belonged to the woman huddled in the corner of the room.

"Stop it!" Piper screamed from her cradled position. "No! You will do as I say," I screamed back.

"Take me instead," Piper offered shakily, "Let him go." "NO," I yelled.

She stood up bravely and approached me. Her trembling form indicated terror, but her face was set in determination. Wanting to illicit a stronger reaction, I pressed the knife along the man's cheek, "STOP IT," she demanded.

"Why should I?" I countered.

"Because you obviously went through all this trouble for me, and I will not stand by and let you harm that innocent man! It's ME you want to kill!"

Releasing the whimpering mortal in my grasp, I stormed toward the star of my production. I swung around and pushed her against the wall where I held my knife close to her neck. "You're right," I admitted. I desperately wanted to force my blade through her flesh and end all of this, but a part of me I couldn't identify protested those thoughts. I was still unable to do it. "But not yet," I backed away and held my weapon out in offering. "Take it," I offered with a nod in the direction of the man strapped to the chair.

"Never will I take another person's life into my hands!"

Her resolution, maddening as it was, proved unbreakable. Knowing under no circumstance would she go through with it, I gave up. Acknowledging my loss, I turned back to the shriveling mess of a man who shrunk away as I approached. *Where was that attitude he had just moments ago?*

Without further ado, I did, as I always did, and created the single humbling gash that would end the little match I'd tried to arrange. It was a pity I had to do it myself when Piper had the opportunity to do so, but I couldn't be too dissatisfied. One way or another, blood was being shed. My eyes trained on the gruesome sight with villainous delight. I watched the life drift away from his body in sync with the expanding sea of red. He shuddered, and then it was finished.

I kicked the chair back and stepped aside as the menacing scarlet river flooded the carpet. I wasn't too bothered by the stains, as I had already considered replacing the flooring in this room anyway. Of course, I would have to do it myself now, but I didn't mind.

Piper dropped to her knees and emptied her stomach at the

sight. As she

wretched, I placed my hand on the small of her back, "It's nothing you haven't seen before," I reminded her of our first encounter. She brushed her dark brown hair out of her face and turned her head. She openly glared at me and made no attempt to hide her hate.

"You're horrible!"

"Nothing new there," I squatted down beside her and lifted her chin with my finger. "I thought you really were going to withhold your hate as you promised."

"You just ended that innocent man's life! How could I not react to that?! It would be hard not to hate you," She got off her knees and rearranged her position so that her back was to the wall and her knees curled up to her chest. She clutched the cross at the end of her necklace tightly and closed her eyes.

Despite the awful smell in the room, I sat down next to her. Whatever emotional revelation about to come would be worth withstanding the metallic scent of blood and acrid stench of vomit.

"I'm awful."

She opened her eyes and I was rewarded by the sight of those beautiful, expressive irises that fueled Cain, "Awful is too light a word to describe you. Your sins are immeasurable."

I tilted my head back and took a deep breath, "Indeed."

"But why? How can you find pleasure in something so horrible?"

It was not something I could easily answer. For whatever reason the blood spatters on my hands did not bring me the peace they usually did. There was nothing pleasurable about that kill. Could her presence have affected me so much that my one true passion has become a hindrance? Just moments ago, I would have relished in any life I took with my own two hands, but now I felt unsettled. Releasing Cain usually allowed for some sense of contentment, but I only felt confused. I left my warring mind to figure it out as I looked at Piper. Her sweet gaze was focused on the window, "You know there will be no escape this time, right?"

"Only in death," she confirmed.

"Do you really believe there is some greater force out there?" I asked. Philosophically, it was a question I had wondered. While I usually dismissed the idea of anything so powerful existing, I wanted to hear her insight.

"Yes," her face was void of the hate from minutes ago.

Maybe I had broken her after all. When I thought that, my chest tightened. The way she acted, along with my inability to even think about adding to the pool of blood in the room, confirmed my mistake. My little show in here had affected her, but just not in the way I had anticipated. If anything, I was the one who suffered. Was it possible that instead of exposing any hidden darkness she could have in order to humanize her, that I was being influenced by her?

I needed to further contemplate those thoughts, but I desired to hear her voice, "Your friend Arial really is something—"

She snorted, "Well, if the killer says so, then it must be true."

Her expression became animated again and I smiled in triumph. *What? Why should I care if she was acting like herself again?* "She's not the brightest, but she let me into her home without question and gave out your location without a thought."

Her face softened, "Aren't you concerned she will lead the police to you if she found anything suspicious?"

"I'm not going to kill her, if that's what you're asking."

She exhaled in relief, "So the name you provided her with was false?"

I manually turned her face with my hand so she would look at me, "No. I really am Sylas Hamell."

Growing bold she asked, "So, Sylas, what's your goal here? What do you think is going to happen?"

"I'm going to find a way to kill you," I answered honestly.

She didn't even flinch, "Why go to all this trouble? Just finish it right here and save yourself the trouble of holding a hostage."

"It's not that simple." I let out a frustrated grunt.

"I beg to differ. You've already killed four, well I guess five now, so you obviously have no trouble with the act itself."

I recounted the past few days and totaled the number in my head, "Eight," I corrected only to realize I had emphasized her point, "As I admitted last time, there is something different about you."

"And then you released me because of that," she added.

"That was a mistake on my part. Look how much trouble I had to go through just to get you back in my possession! I will figure this out, I just needed you to help me—"

"Here I am," she gestured towards herself with the flick of a wrist. Instead of making a remark, I grabbed her arm and pulled her off the ground with me. She was far past struggling as I hauled her into my own bedroom. The window was sealed just like it was in the other room, so there would still be no quick getaway, but I figured it would be more comfortable for her.

There was nothing present that she could use against me in my sleep, so I assumed it would be alright. I grabbed the padlock I stored in my nightstand and attached it around the door handle and a special piece I had added on the frame. I was all about security even if

Stella liked to make fun of it and call my preparations 'kinky.'

"Go ahead and get comfortable," I told Piper, "This is where you'll be staying tonight."

"You're sleeping here too?" she questioned. "Yes."

"But I could easily have the upper hand once you fall asleep."

"You're not the one willing to take that risk," I teased as I went over to the dresser and changed clothes.

She turned away shyly and said, "But I could do it—" "You could, but you won't."

I slipped into the soft, warm comforter of my bed. I was exhausted and nothing sounded better than a good night rest. Piper had opted to sleep on the floor despite my offer of the other half of the bed. Luckily, this room also contained more of the plush carpeting because otherwise it would have been very cold. The more I relaxed the more vulnerable my position became, but I wasn't really concerned. Would she try to get away tonight? Probably. Would she actually succeed? No. I wasn't kidding when I said the only escape would be death, albeit mine or hers. She was too strong in her beliefs, though, to commit what she considered to be an atrocity. She wouldn't kill me and I felt safe in those thoughts as I closed my eyes.

Normally when I fell asleep after a kill, I went to bed feeling exhilarated, fulfilled, and sleep came easily. Tonight however, I felt none of those feelings. Images of death which I had once found so alluring, left me unsettled. *Was I becoming afraid of myself?* The small bit of sleep I did manage, was fitful at best.

The sound of metal clanking woke me. I lifted my head from the pillow groggily to find Piper fiddling with the lock on the door. "A good morning to you too," I stated.

She jumped as my voice startled her, "You're awake."

"So, it would seem. Now, do you happen to be good with locks or are you just trying your very best and hoping for a miracle?"

She dropped the combination lock from between her fingers, "You don't leave me with a lot of options," she grumbled.

"Really? I could have sworn there was a very obvious answer."

"I'm not a killer," she defended, "I don't decide your fate even though I wish I could."

"One punch," I told her as I jumped out of bed. "What?"

"You want the combination," I gestured toward the lock, "One punch equals one number."

She stood up, "Why?"

"Are you really questioning an opportunity to hurt the evil

being that doesn't care about the cost of any life?" Of course, I didn't bring up the point that getting the lock open didn't guarantee her escape. All it did, was free her from this room. Maybe she was aware of it and just wanted space from me.

She stuck her hands into the pockets of her skinny jeans and eyed me thoughtfully, "It doesn't make sense."

"Does it need to?"

"Yes. You only do things that benefit yourself. So, either there's some strange twist or you woke up a different person."

"Well, I would suggest that my sadistic tendencies have reversed drastically but you wouldn't believe that."

She pursed her lips in thought, "You're messing with me," she exclaimed.

"Only one way to find out."

She withdrew her right hand from her pocket and curled her fingers into a tight fist. As she stepped closer, her grasp tightened and the tight ball transformed into an open palm. Then in a move that surprised us both, her fist reformed and slammed into my stomach.

I hadn't braced myself since I expected her to chicken out, so the sucker punch really burned. I took in a ragged breath, "Twelve."

She looked down at her fist guiltily. I didn't think she expected to really hit me either. I grinned. Yesterday, she wouldn't have done something so brazen. Sure, she would have possibly hit me whenever she struggled against my hold, but that was self-defense. This was an unprovoked attack. Or, at least that's how she would see it. Most other people would still consider it defense against a kidnapper, but to her it was more than that. She decided to hurt me. She chose to inflict pain without me having to cause it with a threat of my own.

Looks like this dog does have some bite after all. Even the friendliest dog would act defensively if it thought its owner was in danger, but no sweet puppy would bite the one it had sworn its loyalty to, regardless of what the master commanded. A full-blown bite was something that couldn't be trained. It could be coerced, but not easily asked for. She certainly hadn't pulled that punch either. While it was not the worst I had felt, she had put some weight behind it and my skin still stung below my ribs.

"You need two more numbers if you're going to open that lock."

She looked solemnly toward the door. After a moment of hesitation, two more fists connected. The slap of her hands against my chest echoed throughout the room.

After the first unexpected blow, I braced myself properly.

The tensed muscles over my abdomen provided better padding against her knuckles, but each blow still stung. She shook her hands out loosely as I rewarded her, "Sixteen and thirty."

She rushed over to the lock and turned it to the corresponding spots with shaky hands.

As I rubbed the sore spots where her fists had bruised my flesh, I reminded myself that the way she had reacted was what a human would do. Human. Not dog. I pictured myself knocking her over and wrestling with her until my hands would snake around her throat. While it was still a vision that left me feeling a bit distressed, I could actually see it happening. No longer was it a faraway dream, but a possible reality. Cain rejoiced at this revelation. Slowly but surely, she was changing. Cain was affecting her. She was still untouchable, but now I knew it was possible. I could corrupt her until the point she was just like the rest of the human race. Once I stopped viewing her as innocent and free of the taint of this cruel world, she would finally be more than a fascination. Once I destroyed her perfect nature, she would become prey. Soon the small part of me that wanted to protect her as I did my dogs, would be nothing more than a whisper beside Cain.

With a pop, the lock clicked open. She slid it through its holster and opened the door. Instead of slipping out as she intended, four furry guards blocked her exit. She pushed between the curious mutts and skittered down the hallway.

I paid her no heed as I walked over to the dresser and picked out a change of clothes. A large sweatshirt and some jeans would have to do and I pulled them on as quickly as I could. She knew the consequences of leaving but in case she forgot, I didn't feel like running through the woods since the weather forecast called for potential snow.

When I walked into the main room, I saw something unique. Piper was crouched over the dogs and playing with them. She gave each of them thorough stomach rubs while she cooed in a baby voice.

Great. Just what I need to help her seem less dog and more human.

Seeing her getting along with the only creatures I bothered to create any attachment with gave me an odd feeling inside my stomach. Was this fluttering sensation a sign of nervousness? But why would I be?

"Snow is predicted for this afternoon," I stated casually. She looked up from the dogs to watch me, "And?"

"It would make the terrain outside more difficult to navigate—" "It's a good thing I'm not going outside then," she decided.

81

I looked at her in disbelief, "You really don't want to take any chances with your family, do you?"

She patted Simon's head absent mindedly and returned my gaze, "Escaping here wouldn't accomplish anything. Even if I get out, I'll be on foot and you have a car. You could reach everyone important to me faster than I could arrive to protect them. And if, I, by some miracle, manage to get there first there's a chance I'll be arrested for your crime. In either of those scenarios, my family and friends are at risk and I'm not there to help. If I have to be away from them, I might as well be somewhere I can guarantee they won't be harmed."

She had really put some thought into this. I just assumed that self-preservation would win out against logic. It would appear I was wrong, but I was not bitter over being proven so. In fact, it was a relief to know that she wouldn't be going anywhere.

"Interesting thoughts. So, you're only staying here to keep an eye on me then?"

"If you're stuck watching me, that's time you aren't using against my loved ones."

I whistled and the dogs, which were lazily sprawled on the floor, stood up. Alert ears erected and eyes looked to me for a command. "Daisy, out. Rebel, out. Simon, out. Buster, out."

Piper looked around in amazement as the beasts scampered off to the back door and exited through the dog flap in an organized manner, "They're well trained," she commented.

"I have a way with dogs," I replied with a wink. "Knives too."

I laughed as she stood up and waltzed into the kitchen, "Are you getting something to eat?" I asked as I followed right behind her.

"I can eat, right?"

"Of course. Starvation is so boring," I opened the drawer that contained the silverware and grabbed a butter knife. It was too dull to do much damage, but after swinging it around in the air a few times she understood the message.

She made a small plate of toast and nibbled on in mindlessly, while sitting on one of the bar stools along the island.

I made some coffee for myself and leaned against the counter as I slowly drained my cup. Neither of us said a word as we embraced the comforting silence. From an outsiders' perspective, it would have appeared that nothing was wrong. We could have easily been mistaken for a couple casually eating breakfast. The truth, however, was much more sinister. I was a killer and across from me sat the woman I had kidnapped and kept under my roof at the threat of harming her family.

Chapter 10

"So, why dogs?" I asked him at last as I picked at the last slice of toast on my plate. I wasn't hungry enough to finish it, and it provided something for my trembling hands to do.

He looked up from his coffee mug with a thoughtful expression. "What's wrong with my dogs?"

"Nothing," I answered shyly. "But it's the last thing I thought a serial killer would have to keep himself company."

He shrugged. " They are loyal and make good guards," he answered simply.

"I just thought that murderers lacked the empathy needed to own such pets. I thought people like you would kill them for sport." It was something that had been on my mind ever since I saw the pooches strolling around his property. I had once heard that the first acts of violence true psychotic killers performed were usually against small, helpless critters.

"People like me?" He put his cup down and waltzed over to the island where I was seated. He placed his elbows on the counter and stared at me deeply. "There aren't other people like me. I'm a unique specimen. You're right, though; most killers would slay anything that moved, but I'm different. I only enjoy killing what I hate."

"You have to hate something to kill it?" I inquired.

"Yes."

"But how could you possible hate all those people you killed? Weren't they strangers?"

He laughed, "It's not individual people I hate, but humanity as a whole. When I was a boy, I didn't easily get along with others and as Cain began to manifest, I started to have fantasies," he said as he delved into his memories, "What if I cut my obnoxious neighbor? Would he cry as he bled? Would he beg for mercy at my hands? I never acted on any of those thoughts and pushed it aside. I thought it was just a phase, but he never left. Instead of wanting to see someone die, I desired for it to be with my own two hands. There was this dark whisper, Cain, that didn't concern himself with the likes of others and wanted to massacre everyone."

One portion of his speech struck me oddly, "Cain?" I queried.

He froze at my interruption. He bit his lower lip between his teeth in contemplation. His hesitation to answer confirmed my suspicion. I assumed that detail had been a slip of the tongue rather than intentional disclosure. Either way, it appeared important. If I was to understand any portion of my situation, I couldn't skim past Sylas' past.

After a momentary pause, Sylas resumed speaking, "Cain. I named him Cain. It was as if a part of me had broken and this alternate side formed, and it made sense to give it its own identity. Cain is a part of me, the part that loves to kill."

I was absorbed in his morbid tale and even though it was horrible, I couldn't turn away. As much as I hated the man before me, I was also very curious. I wanted to know how he became the way he was. I had to know. "How old were you when you had those thoughts?" I asked for clarification.

"When I realized I was different? Seven. When I realized that the obsession with murder would become more than that? I don't know when that happened, honestly, but it was younger than you'd imagine."

I gaped at his response.

"And when I was seventeen, my father was lying in a pool of his own blood."

I scooched my chair back. *Holy cow!* As unforgiveable as it was to kill someone; it was a whole other level of sin to take the life of your own flesh and blood.

He looked at me intensely. "I didn't kill him."

"What?" Now I was confused. I should have stopped listening then, but

I was too engulfed in his story to walk away.

"Someone else beat me to it. It was a mugger who cut him down while he was at home by himself. My mother and sister were overcome by grief, but I—didn't care," he said through clenched teeth, "I should have felt bad, but all I felt was relief that I wasn't the one who had done it. I was too young to get away with it, but my need for blood had become so unbearable and, since he was the easiest target, it was just a matter of time. My sister was in so much pain after it all happened and I had almost been the reason. I'm not an emotional person, I hardly feel anything, in fact, but it felt so wrong to stand back and watch her sweet, trusting nature disappear. She was like you once. I couldn't have harmed her when she was younger–she was too innocent and a part of me had wanted to protect her."

"What happened to her?" I asked. If it was true that I was replicating whatever his sister was, then I might be able to stop him from killing me or at least buy myself some more time.

84

"She grew up," he said so softly that it almost sounded as if there was genuine sadness behind his words. His face, as always, remained an unbreakable mask. The only two emotions that had broken through that exterior were anger and triumph and I'd only witnessed those when he killed.

"Well, I'm grown myself," I added. It might have been stupid to point that out in case it could be used against me, but I was seeking answers. "Puppies grow into dogs. I can't kill dogs."

"Why am I the only one you perceive as a dog?"

He straightened out his back and rubbed a hand over his face. A bit of blonde stubble had formed along his mouth and he scratched at it, "It's probably because your exposure to humanity hasn't darkened you in any way. You stick to your beliefs and remain selfless even in spite of everything. The only other creature I can think of with those same characteristics is a dog and since I have a strange fondness for canines; it makes it hard to harm you."

"But you wish to harm me." "Yes."

"But to do that, you need to find a way to humanize me. You think if you can associate some of the emotions that make you hate people with me that you will be able to kill me?" I asked as the puzzle pieces locked together. This was why he had asked me to hit him earlier. He was trying to make himself hate me.

"You're a smart one," he complimented even if it was done humorously, "Now," he began as he pushed up the sleeves of his sweatshirt, "I have a body to take care of."

"You're despicable," I spat.

"I am, but I'm okay with that," he continued down the hallway toward the room where he had killed the man from last night. I looked as he returned with a body in tow. He dragged it down the hallway and lifted it over his shoulder.

"This is why I kill outside my house so I don't have to deal with the cleanup," he grumbled before he opened the back door and headed into the wilderness. A cold wind swept through the house as he closed the door. I shivered at the sudden chill and looked through the window to see his back disappear into the line of trees. If it was supposed to snow maybe he would be trapped outside if I decided to lock him out when it happened. I immediately dismissed that cruel thought. I shouldn't be wishing bad things on anyone no matter what they had done. I was not the one who made those decisions.

I clamped the precious pendant that hung around my neck. It was the only thing that reminded me that there was more to this. While he might think he was alone in his evil, there was always someone else seeing his actions and when the day came; he would pay for what he had done.

Having heard his story, though, I admitted there was more to it than met the eye. What he had done and would, unfortunately, continue to do was unforgivable. What he told me in no way excused that, but it did make things more complicated. *Is his sanity even intact?* I questioned whether this Cain could be the cause of something medical, but quickly dismissed it. He was too aware of everything and intelligent enough that he would have known if that was the case.

I felt something brush against my leg and looked down to see the small black and white dog standing at my side.

"Hey there," I spoke softly. The dog tilted her head curiously in response to my voice. I looked into the sweet eyes of the beautiful dog. How could such an innocent creature have any love for such a terrible owner? I guess because he was only cruel to everyone except for the dogs that had accepted him.

I looked down into the gentle face of the loving dog and scrubbed my hands across her face. "Good girl," I coaxed and her tail wagged in response. It was amusing to see the way she reacted. I had seen and played with dogs before, but I had never had the chance to have one growing up. My father, although a good man, was a bit strict. He had never allowed me to have any pets because he was afraid they would distract me from more important things, like school and church. While I had always held a bit of a grudge about it, I had still never gotten any companions of my own. While I lived by myself now and could afford one, there had never been a good time to get one. My apartment had been small, grimy, and I wanted to wait until I had a larger space.

I stood up beside the happy dog and commanded, "Sit," nothing happened. Tongue lolled out of her mouth, the mutt looked up at me with a glint in her animal eyes, "Sit," I repeated more firmly. Recognition flared across the dog's face and I could have sworn she understood what I said, but she remained on four legs. "Sit," I asked one more time and moved my hand up to aid her in the motion. Still nothing. Tail loosely flailed behind her, the dog barked. Either she was being defiant or she was challenging me.

"Daisy, sit," a deep voice rumbled behind me. Startled, I nearly jumped out of my skin at the sudden interruption. I looked back to see Sylas standing a few feet away. When I looked back, the dog's hindquarters magically touched the floor. She was sitting.

"Your dogs' aren't as well trained as you thought," I mumbled.

"Quite the contrary," he countered, "Daisy, down." Without

missing a beat, Daisy slammed her front limbs into the ground until her back was flat, "She only responds to commands when you use her name," he clarified upon seeing my confusion.

"Daisy, sit," I ordered. This time she pushed against the ground while keeping her hind legs in place and once again in the sitting position. I clapped my hands together enthusiastically.

He laughed and his voice opened up musically, "Enjoying yourself?" He snagged a stool from around the island and took a seat.

"I've never done that before," I admitted.

"Don't lie. If I recall, this is the second time I've kidnapped you." I wasn't even going to address that, "I meant the dog."

"I'm sure you've seen a dog before. Sure, you're a bit sheltered, but they're not a very rare resource." He was well aware what I meant, but chose to keep making me correct him. It was as if he was purposely drawing out the conversation. I had noticed him doing it before in our previous talks, but I had written it off as actual confusion. He was watching me with a certain intensity from his perch on the seat and I had to pry my gaze away to refocus.

"Of course, I've seen dogs before, but I've never had the opportunity to give one a command before. It's so cool how they listen!"

"I agree. Training them, though time consuming, was a rewarding experience."

I turned so that my back faced him. I bent over and granted Daisy a few more affectionate pats, "So, what now?" I asked without turning around, "Do you have a plan for the day or are you just going to continue observing me?" In truth, he wasn't the only one that made observations. I was, admittedly, a bit fascinated with him. The way his mind worked was unlike anything I had seen before and, although the situation was awful, it would make the situation a unique experience. When we started talking, I learned that he was very open. Being the self-acclaimed anti-social man he was, I knew that the details I learned in our discussions were things he wouldn't easily tell others. Why he revealed such thoughts was a mystery all in its own, but I suspected he did it to gain my trust. Not the real type of trust that allowed a pair to have faith in each other, but the kind that tempted me to reveal my own secrets. For whatever it was worth, it appeared he was just as fascinated with me. We were complete opposites in both nature and beliefs and that created a shock value when our opinions clashed.

He sighed, "I was just wondering the same thing. I had planned this around the idea that things would have gone differently last night."

"You assumed there wasn't going to be a second day with

me."

I craned my neck in time to see his gentle shrug, "Maybe I was asking for too much. You're still a work in progress."

So, I was still a ticking bomb. "I don't know what you think would ever cause me to forget everything I was brought up learning, but just know I will not cave in from my ideals."

"Everyone has a breaking point. I'll just have to find a way to make you decompose from the inside out. You will succumb to my ways eventually. The major difference between us is that I'm evil. That means mercy and guilt will never be present. You'd be wise to remember that."

"Good always prevails," I retorted defiantly.

He jumped off the small stool and towered over me, "And that's where you have yet to feel the dark mark society imprints upon us. If you really believe that is true then you still have a lot to learn."

"You are wrong." "You're naïve."

I stood up and moved until we were close enough I could feel his warm breath upon every exhale. He was much taller and the top of my head just barely reached his muscular chest. I tilted my head in order to gain his undivided attention, "What's wrong with believing there is something better out there?"

He scoffed, "It's irrational."

"No, it's not! You have no proof that there isn't something worth believing in!"

"Exactly. There is no proof."

I clenched my hands into fists at my sides and glared at him, "Don't twist my words. You know exactly what I mean!"

He lowered his head so it was level with mine. His icy irises flared a passionate blue, "I'm a killer. I gain immeasurable pleasure in taking away something as precious as life. I would kill my whole family without batting an eye. And guess what? I would savor every moment of it. How can you put so much faith in your deliverer of peace when my very existence contradicts that notion?"

I gulped, "We aren't supposed to know everything. The mysteries about our existence aren't something we were made to solve."

"I exist to cease humanity's existence. I was made to kill."

"No, you weren't! No one is born to kill. You've taken fate in your own hands and you cannot blame your sins on something else!"

His hand lifted up and his fingers feathered across my neck. They stopped at a vital point and I felt his index finger nudge my carotid artery. He pushed in a little and my pulse rammed into his finger, "Then why does my touch cause such atrocities?" he asked in a whisper as his head leaned in, and he spoke directly into my ear, "Tell me why I get such a high from causing pain. Tell me why all I can think about is your pretty face smiling not in life but in death," His touch retreated and he backed away.

"I don't have those answers," I informed him.

"Yet, you are the key. The man I murdered last night? I felt none of the usual euphoria and you are the reason why."

"What?" I was stunned at his admittance.

"I trained my dogs using positive reinforcement. It feels wrong to punish them."

"So, we're back to that again," I said dryly.

He ignored what I intended to be interpreted as sarcasm, "That's why I need you to stop being innocent. I can't kill you as a dog. And I *need* to kill you. You seem to be affecting the level of satisfaction I gain from spilling blood and I certainly can't have that."

This was not good. It would appear I created another vendetta for him to hold against me. If I really interfered with his kills, then he would only be further encouraged to end things quickly. My time was running shorter every second.

"But in the mean-time?" I inquired.

He rubbed the back of his neck, "I guess we will accompany each other. There's not much else. I was foolish enough to assume my plan would work so I apologize if it's a bit boring."

It was so silly to hear him concerned about my level of engagement, "You're apologizing in case I get bored?"

He ran his long fingers though his lustrous hair. "Oh, I don't know. I've never mae mistakes as critical as this! I allowed too much room for error and now I'm paying the price." For someone so controlling, it must have been difficult to have his miscalculations rubbed in his face.

A buzzing from his pocket brought our attention to his phone. He sighed and paused our discussion temporarily as he checked the screen. His fingers tapped furiously along the small smartphone and I found myself curious as to whom he replied to. It was no secret he was texting, but I had no guesses as to who the second party could be.

"What is it?" I asked quietly.

The way he stared at me indicated he didn't want to answer but still did so, "My sister, Stella."

"Your sister? I, um, thought—"

"You assumed I don't bother communicating with anyone else because of how awful I am."

"Well, I figured this kind of stuff," I said as I recreated a stabbing motion with my hands, "Causes a bit of a familial drift."

"Don't write me off as a fool. You are the only one who knows about it and that is solely because I don't plan on letting you live any longer than necessary," his voice was clipped and his face held a certain ferocity.

I must have been so accustomed to his threats of killing me because I didn't even flinch at his statement, "So why is she contacting you?" I prodded. "Do you have any siblings?"

"No. I'm an only child."

"Then you won't understand. Count yourself lucky you've never had to deal with a nosey sister," he stopped as his gaze raked over my frozen form, "One of a kind," he whispered under his breath so quietly I almost missed it.

"I don't know. I think you're the lucky one. Someone out there genuinely cares for you, even if you aren't necessarily deserving of it," I commented while ignoring his previous statement, which I assumed wasn't meant for me to hear.

"Because all I ever wanted in life is to be cuddled," he stated in a tone dripping with sarcasm.

"You might not feel emotions the way the rest of us do, but you should at least appreciate the gesture," I scolded.

"I don't need advice on how to manage my social connections. I've lived long enough to fake what I need to, and that includes emotions," He dropped to his knees suddenly and gripped my hips. "Oh, Piper please," he cried, "Don't let my condemned soul stop you from loving me." While his words and over dramatization gave away the act; I did have to admit, it was somewhat convincing. His skills also extended to acting, it would seem. *I bet he cries crocodile tears.*

I pried his hands from my side, "Very funny. I wonder if that's how any of your victims acted so they could make you feel good," I knew I had taken it too far as he inhaled a shaky breath. His hands trembled. Gone were his good- natured remarks and now his more sinister side surfaced. *Could this be Cain?*

His hands reached down and swept my feet out from under me. My head hit the marble floor with a crack and a sharp pain shot up my skull. Before I could move away he had crawled over me, placed his hands along my wrists and knees, and his knee in-between my legs to prevent any motion. His body covered mine and every small movement was met with strong resistance.

"Make no mistake," he hissed in my face, "Each and every one of my victims felt the crushing amount of terror you will soon feel yourself. Don't think this current predicament means anything in regard to if you will die. It's a matter of when. My face will be the last one you see before you are consumed by eternal darkness.

Memorize it, until every pore strikes fear into your delicate being and let it haunt you at night."

I was shaking. It was hard not to be frightened by his intimidating presence, but I knew I had to retaliate, "If death is my escape, why should I fear it?"

His fingers dug into my skin, "You misinterpreted my words. It's an escape for me. Without you, I can return to what I was," His teeth scraped across my neck and continued upward until his mouth was positioned at my cheek. He moved his head away when he reached the bandage covering my cut, "Death will garner you no peace. Whatever you think is waiting for you on the other side doesn't exist. You will be greeted by nothing other than the darkness consistent with death. I will be there as your very existence fades away and do you know what your last thoughts will be?"

I turned my head away and refused to listen.

"Do you know what your last thoughts will be?" he asked loudly. I jerked my head around in response, "Do you know what they will be?" he repeated with more volume, "You will be wondering why I was smiling."

I faced him head on, "I have no need to think about that. I'll know why you are smiling." For the sake of the scenario he painted in my head, I assumed that he was going to kill me. I still had faith that it would work out by some miracle, but I played along anyways to give him piece of my mind.

"No, you won't."

"You're going to smile because you love killing and somewhere in that condemned soul of yours, you're going to rejoice at the sight of blood."

He flashed a set of perfect, white teeth, "That's what you don't get. I enjoy what I do, yes, but I don't smile. As I drain the life from my victims, I frown. I love killing, but I don't want them to understand that. Killing them happily, while not ideal for them, makes them think there was some purpose behind their death. While it does indeed satisfy me, they will never know. I like making them feel insignificant right before they pass. My smile is reserved for you," his voice dropped to a deeper, more beveled tone.

"But why?"

"That's what you'll be wondering as I leave you to bleed," he swiped his tongue across his top row of teeth."

"You're a monster," I cried.

"Didn't we understand this revelation long ago?" He rebuffed rhetorically.

He kept me pushed to the ground, but released my arms from his vice grip. I unfurled my fingers and flinched as the circulation returned and pumped against the numb appendages. His weight on top of mine was enough to keep me restrained. While I was still in such a vulnerable position, he reached up and ripped the bandage from my cheek. I winced at the speed at which he removed it, for it irritated the sensitive area. He rubbed a finger over the wound with a single digit and traced over the small raised sutures.

"You got stitches," he said bluntly while he inspected the mark.

"Three days ago, yes," I recalled being at Arial's place when I realized how bad the cut had been. I had fretted about what I overheard at the police station when I found myself pacing in front of the bathroom mirror. It was the first chance I had seen myself after the initial ordeal. I removed the Band-Aid to examine it when Arial walked in. One look at the gaping skin on my face had her driving me to the Emergency room in a flash.

"Hmm," he mumbled and I couldn't tell if it was a sound of displeasure or not. He removed his hand and stood up. Finally relieved from his crushing force, I sat up. I cradled the back of my head with my palm and looked up to meet his stare. His arms were crossed as he observed my every move. I eyed him from my position on the ground.

With a grunt, he left me alone to analyze what had just happened.

Chapter 11

My phone had buzzed nonstop since I left the room. Apparently, Stella was so bored that I had become her only source of entertainment. I was having a very serious moment with Piper and she had to interrupt with her persistent messages. My mood soured as I read through her texts. They were all saying hello and asking what I was doing. Certainly nothing worth interrupting my time with Piper. I turned off the phone and slipped it into my pocket. Stella's rambling could wait, but my time with the mysterious woman in my living room was limited.

I had been vicious and I could tell she was fearful, but she still managed to face me head on. Her willingness to challenge me was so unexpected that I had refrained from mocking the absurdity. She just kept surprising me and I felt a bit glad that I couldn't quite kill her yet. She was so intriguing that I had grown to look forward to being in her company. While it did nothing to change my opinion on what must happen to her, it made things more interesting.

Out of the corner of my eye, I noticed something moving by the window. I turned to see the first icy flurries that began to fall. I wandered over to the window and pressed my face against the cold glass and watched with childish wonder as the small, white specks fluttered to the ground. It was nothing I hadn't seen before, but it was always an amazing sight to watch the first snowfall of the year. When I had checked the forecast only a few measly inches were predicted. The clouds would pass soon after they deposited their cold fluff. I sighed and watched as my exhale fogged up the window. I couldn't resist taking a finger and drawing a smiley face through the temporary patch of condensation.

With one last glance at the whimsical show, I exited the bedroom and headed down the narrow hallway. Making my way into the main room, I found Piper looking through the glass panes of the back door with a look that mirrored the one I had just donned. I guess I wasn't the only one who appreciated the beautiful weather.

She noticed my presence when I was a few feet away even though I remained silent. Without acknowledgment she spoke wistfully, "Not a bad way to go. With such pretty scenery, it's hard to imagine anything bad could happen." I thought about that juxtaposition myself. Evil was often hidden in beauty, "It's hard to dig when the ground is that cold."

Piper jumped to the side just in time for the dog door to burst open. Daisy scampered inside and shook out her pelt. Small droplets of water flung across the room. After she had rid herself of the snowflakes, Daisy ran up to me and skidded to a halt behind my leg.

"She's shaking!" Piper exclaimed worriedly.

"Not everyone appreciates the snow," I placed a hand on the dog's head reassuringly. "She's always been afraid of the stuff. The other dogs love rolling around in the snow, but she seems to avoid it at all costs."

Piper frowned, "Poor dog," she crouched down and extended her hand. Daisy poked her head out slowly and gave her hand a curious sniff. Sensing nothing dangerous, Daisy slinked forward until she was curled into Piper's arms. Piper smoothed her coat comfortingly and cooed calming words to Daisy. The dog visibly relaxed in her hold, "She likes you," I noted.

"Don't you dare make a comment about me being one of them."

"Unfortunately, getting a dog to like you doesn't require being as innocent as one of them," I motioned back to myself. "Cats on the other hand—" "Is that why you hate cats?"

I nodded, "They're too smart for their own good. Dogs will befriend anyone, but cats are much more selective over who receives their trust."

"Hmm."

"What?" I asked.

She bit her lower lip and continued to stroke Daisy's pelt with care, "Well, if I'm a dog, then you are a cat."

"I hate cats."

"But you said you hated humans and yet you are one of them. It makes sense when you think about it. Cats are similar to dogs yet they deviate from them in some fundamental way."

"So, until I can make you just another rat, I'm a cat trying to hunt a dog."

She turned away from the window so that I could get a view of her face. "That's an interesting way of thinking about it. When you put it like that, though, it sounds like I have all the power in this situation. Any reasonable-sized dog could easily overpower a cat."

I coughed out a laugh. "Maybe I'm not a housecat, but a lion."

"Well, your morals definitely reflect that of something undomesticated."

I was thinking of a clever response, but what interrupted

with a whimper from Daisy. There was only one way to help a frightened dog. I headed over to the kitchen and fetched a filled rawhide bone from one of the vast number of cabinets. When I returned, her ears were already perked and her tail had dislodged itself from between her legs and was wagging in a slow rhythm. I held the irresistible treat out to the canine and she grabbed it greedily with her teeth. She ran off to her favorite spot on the couch to enjoy her delicacy in peace.

Piper stood up and brushed her hands on her jeans. "I'll never understand it. How can you be so gentle one moment and then merciless the next?"

I tapped a finger along my chin, "If I had that answer, neither of us would be here. "

"Some things are more than meets the eye."

"That would appear to be true about both of us," I offered. "The small details, though, make things appear more complicated so it's best not to look too far into them."

"I already know what I need to about you. You are a killer. I never said that any of those subtle facts influenced that conclusion. But the way you are is, admittedly, interesting. None of it can excuse your awful behavior, but its makes something so unfathomable yet somewhat understandable. I don't condone your sins, but I do find it thought provoking to learn the driving force behind it all."

I blinked. As much as she hated me; she was willing to confess I piqued her interest. The same could be said about my thoughts toward her. We were both such opposites, her a reflection of light and me a mirror of darkness, that it was only natural we sought answers to the other's existence. We were both shocked at the other's methods and principles that we couldn't help but wait for the other to discuss it.

I locked my gaze onto her soft, brown eyes as I strode forward. She didn't move as I curled my finger around a strand of her dark hair. Her eyes shimmered against her creamy, porcelain complexion. When I was this close to another human it usually meant I was about to begin a reign of slaughter but, as I remained inches away from this puppy, I felt no such urge. It was like when I saw her for the first time in that apartment. I was granted a rare reprieve from Cain. In this fleeting moment, I felt almost human. With Cain silenced, even for the shortest measure of time, I was freed from him. But was it a good thing? I felt exposed without him circulating through my brain. Did I want them to return or was it just the discomfort from something unfamiliar?

Although Cain was suppressed, the thoughts of curiosity didn't fade, "Keep talking," I urged.

Chapter 12

It was the oddest feeling and something I had not experienced since I first saw Sylas spill the blood of my neighbor. I was overwhelmed with a sense of calm. *Inches away from a killer and I felt...Comfortable?* Something was definitely wrong with me if I was able to relax in his grasp. He moved his hand from my hair and took a step back as if affected by some unseen force. When I looked at him, he looked confused, but it was more than that, though. Something else about his presence was different. His normally cold, blue eyes softened and his harsh frown loosened.

"Keep talking," he demanded in a voice I didn't recognize. "Why?"

"Because I've told you so much about me, yet there's so much to explore about you."

I gawked when I realized he was serious, "Do you always become this acquainted with your victims?"

"Do you always become this comfortable with your kidnappers?" he countered.

I straightened my posture, startled by his accusation. For some odd reason I *was* comfortable, but he needn't know that, "But I don't understand why."

His right hand swept through his golden hair, "You admitted it yourself. We already know all we need to know about each other: I'm a killer and you're my next victim, but that doesn't mean the insignificant details can't provide some perspective. Plus, there's nothing else to do out here."

I turned and saw that within the time we talked, a thin layer of snow had coated the ground, "Alright," I agreed hesitantly.

His ruggedly handsome face lit with a smile. It was an odd look on him.

It was the first genuine grin he emitted and it softened his image a fraction. It sure beat that sinister look he got when he discussed what he did to his prey.

I moved toward the black leather sofa and took a seat next to Daisy. He took a seat in the matching loveseat. His arms dangled across the plush armrests as he assumed a relaxed position. I crossed my legs neatly over the expensively upholstered couch. One of my hands came to rest in my lap while the other reached out to

Daisy. The dog was so absorbed in her bone, she barely acknowledged our intrusion.

He spoke first, "Do you have any, uh, hobbies?"

I shook my head, "I tried cooking, but unfortunately my only talent is grilled cheese. Anything else I seem to burn or undercook," it felt so wrong to be talking so casually, when I thought what could happen at any time.

"I guess we share one thing in common then. I can't cook for sh—" I coughed to interrupt any foul language.

He shook his head, "Different worlds," he muttered in disbelief.

"We're not from different worlds, but we choose to live in separate ones. We both started from the same place, but ended up somewhere completely different."

"That's one way of thinking about it. But I didn't choose this, I've merely embraced it."

"You submitted to temptation," I surmised.

He moved his arms so that they rested above his knees and his head was supported by his hands, "This is not a matter of eating one too many cookies," he reiterated. "This is no mere craving. If it was just that, not only would it have been much easier to resist, but it would have only been a fleeting phase that left me wracked with guilt. This is much more than that. It is an all-consuming need. I've always been different. I've never felt the things you have and the only true feeling of happiness I get comes from something so awful I can't even talk about without signing away my own life. The worst part? I don't even care about that. I should feel something, but I'm barren inside. I could care less what happens to others. Cain is so deeply rooted within me that he is the only thing that will never leave. My dogs will eventually die. Cain is a part of me and I love him for it."

"Have you ever tried to ignore him?"

He laughed, "He's not someone who can easily be ignored," as a weird expression passed over his face. "He never leaves," there was something ominous about the way he said the last part that I wondered if he was hiding something.

"If you die?"

"He will follow me," he confirmed. "Death is the only escape," I echoed.

He lifted his head, "No one will get that opportunity," he growled. His voice was strong, but it did lack the ferocity he had earlier.

"Not even me?"

"You couldn't do it," He was certain in his words and he had every right to be. I knew myself and I was not capable of such an atrocity, "You're not capable of causing my death."

"Seeing all that you've done, I kind of regret that I can't," I thought back to Sylas' victims. All of them had suffered at his hands. He had caused more pain in a matter of weeks than most caused in their entire life. Such a monster shouldn't be allowed to exist, but I wasn't capable of executing him. While most would break after so much stress and be able to forget their own moral boundaries long enough to save themselves, I wasn't part of that crowd.

Although in my case it was for the better, I was an outlier in society like he was. His differences allowed him to kill someone without second thought, while mine made it impossible to do the same no matter how much I thought about it. Ridding the world of Sylas would benefit many and save numerous others, but I couldn't do it.

He laughed, "My inner self, Cain, manifests as a beast but yours must be an angel."

"I'm no angel. I've made mistakes in my life too so don't go off the assumption that I'm perfect because it's untrue."

"You? What have you done? Cheated at a game of monopoly?" He laughed even harder.

I squirmed in my seat, "You know what I mean."

He regained his composure and nodded, "Of course. But when I compare what you consider to be bad against my actions, you have to admit you look pretty perfect." His cool gaze swooped over me, "Besides, you're the closest thing to an angel I'll meet in my lifetime."

"And you are the closest I'll ever come to the Devil."

His lips quirked upward, "Now you're getting it. We were made to cancel each other out. We're born enemies."

"I don't think you understand what an angel is." "A peaceful being," he tried.

"Sort of."

"And as the Devil who brought hate and evil, the two would be locked in an eternal power struggle."

"Yes, but angels don't have enemies," I was trying to be patient but I wasn't a fan of his implications.

"But I'm your enemy," he argued.

I found myself tapping my fingers along the denim of my pants, "But

I'm not an angel so that shouldn't be a part of the argument."

He shrugged in surrender, "If that's really what you believe, then fine." "Why do you always feel the need to question my beliefs?" I asked.

Suddenly, the necklace hanging around my throat felt heavier and I was instantly aware of it.

"For the same reason, you keep asking about me. I don't get it," Sylas leaned back in his seat. His hands were interlocked behind his head as he reclined.

"But you don't need to understand it."

"If I want to know more about you then, yes I do." He wasn't even focused on me anymore. He stared past me to the window as he watched the snow continue to flutter down, "I'm failing to see the benefits behind all of it. With my desires comes pleasure. I fail to see where your belief in a separate entity has helped you."

My narrow fingers began to work the necklace. I was rubbing the small cross back and forth across my hand, "Not everything is so selfish. Rewards aren't always instant nor should they be."

"But what if you spend all this time showing your devotion only to find out at the end of your days that it was a waste?"

I should have been offended by his question, but when he looked at me I could tell it was not his intention. He was truly clueless and unlike a normal person, he didn't grasp these things well. I answered calmly, "Although I sincerely doubt what you say is true. *If* you are correct, then it will still have all been worth it. With my faith, there is a certain level of fulfillment and security that allows me to really treasure life."

"So, you'd give in to such strict boundaries and force yourself to do all of that for a sense of security?" He arched a blonde eyebrow.

"I need it," I confessed. "Why?"

I took a deep breath and then shared all my thoughts on the subject, "The world is a much nicer place than you paint it to be. It does, however, still have its flaws. There is corruption and, as I've now seen, evil. Those types of acts can make it hard to go on. Seeing the bad things people are capable of, is horrifying. How can I justify living in such a place where our society has so many injustices that it's appalling? Some people cope with that by either ignoring these issues or becoming a part of them. For me, it's different. The only way I can keep going forward with a bright attitude, is by believing there is higher power out there balancing the scales in the favor of good, is reassuring. Having these beliefs allow me to go to sleep at night, knowing that no one is above their actions. I like to think there is something out there to grant us equality in the most intimate of places. Death."

He nodded his head slowly as he took it all in, "For you,

it's not a matter of wanting there to be something better out there, but needing it."

"Yes," I released the cross pendant from between my fingers and readjusted my hands on my lap.

"Piper."

At the sound of my name, I lifted my gaze from my lap, "Yes." "That's why I will smile for you."

"I don't understand," My brows furrowed as I tried to figure out what he meant.

"What you just told me confirmed my thoughts about you. You are different and therefore deserve better than to be slain by my cruel hands. That's why, when you are in the throes of death, I will smile. I want to send you off with an image of something better. You deserve more than a cruel frown."

My chance to reply was interrupted as the sound of the front door opened. Sylas jumped, while I tensed.

"Sylas!" a feathery voice called, "Are you home?"

"Crap," Sylas muttered as a petite blond woman came into view.

I didn't even need to have seen her before I knew who it was. With a tall frame, shockingly bright hair, and icy blue eyes; she strongly resembled her brother.

"Stella, what are you doing here?" he demanded with a groan. Stella placed her hand on her hip, "Checking in on you."

"You could have texted or given me some warning."

She raised a brow and adapted a smug expression, "I did. You weren't answering your phone, though."

He reached a hand into his pocket before retracting it and rubbing a hand down his face. She peered around her brother's broad chest, "Who is that?" she asked while looking at me with an exact replica of the eyes that haunted my dreams.

I had no idea what to say in this situation. Should I reveal that he was keeping me captive and hoping she would help me or remain silent on the chance she would side with her brother? If the interaction they had was any indication, they were close. Sylas had admitted that Stella didn't know about his less than desirable activities, but there was no telling how she would react. She seemed loyal enough to defend her brother unfortunately. Most people were willing to protect their loved ones, even at the cost of others.

She looked at me expectantly, but my throat suddenly went dry. Sylas butted in, "She's a friend."

Her estranged expression didn't lighten, "Really?" "Am I not allowed to have company over?"

Stella slapped him playfully on the shoulder, "You hate

company."

Daisy seemed to decide that the new person deserved her attention more than her bone as she jumped off the couch, and rushed over to greet the newest intruder. Stella lowered herself to the dog's level and frazzled her face between her hands.

"How did you get in?" Sylas asked before he walked off to the other side of the house. He clicked and locked the front door again before he returned to us.

In that time, Stella eyed me suspiciously. She assumed a stiff posture and decided to focus more on the dog than anything else. It would appear she was just as uncomfortable with my presence, as I was with hers. Maybe she was just as introverted as her brother without all the side effects.

"You have me a spare key," she answered when Sylas stood over her again.

"As I recall, it was less of a gift and more of you just deciding to take it," he corrected with annoyance.

She dismissed him with a wave of her hand. "But seriously, who is she?"

He jerked his head in my direction, "That is, as I said before, my friend, Piper."

Stella pressed her hands down the material of her fashionable sweater in an attempt to smooth the fabric. Her UGG boots covered her small feet, which she shifted nervously. "You don't have any friends."

I wanted to laugh at her statement, but decided to bite my tongue. There was no need to get in between the two siblings. Sylas motioned in my direction. "I definitely have some, unlike someone."

Stella stomped her foot in a pout. "I have some friends."

Sylas rolled his eyes. "Uh-huh."

"I avoid people because I want to. Not the other way around. I could make more friends if I wanted to," she clarified.

Sylas didn't respond and allowed the conversation to drop. I knew whose side Stella would take if she knew the truth. She was not going to be my savior in all of this so it was best to maintain the act Sylas expected of me.

Stella stpped closer and I stood up from the couch. She extended her hand and I shook it, "It's nice to meet you, Piper."

"And I, you."

"It's Stella," she corrected.

"Nice to meet you, Stella," I tested her name.

She nodded then turned back to Sylas, "So where did you find this one?" she asked.

"It's a long story," he deflected.

She plopped down into the chair where he had previously been sitting, "I have time."

"No, you don't," he growled. "You've checked in and seeing as I'm not dead, your job is done."

Stella pointed to the window, "It's snowing outside. You know I don't do well driving in poor weather conditions. Don't force me to go just yet, Sy."

"You are bad driving in any weather conditions," he agreed.

I cleared my throat, "She did drive all the way here. The least you could do is let her stay a while," I interjected. Stella smiled as I jumped to her defense and I was glad I had earned some brownie points. When I first saw her, I was worried she would act cold toward me, but that was not the case.

"'A little while quickly becomes a multiple day stay with this one," Sylas warned. If she did stay over, he would have a fun time explaining my constant presence.

"I'll be gone before sunrise," she promised. "But what sunrise?" Sylas pushed.

"Tomorrow morning, okay?" She spoke volumes with her hands as each gesture emphasized her thoughts, "Geez, I'm even offering to leave before breakfast. Not many guys would argue with that."

Sylas' fingers worked at his temples, "Do you want me to kick you out right now?"

She let out a shrill laugh, "You're a bit tense, bro. You need to relax.

You're still technically on vacation."

"Fine. You can stay in my room for the night."

"Your room? No, I can only infringe so much. Besides, I'm sure the guest room is cozy enough in this giant house of yours.

The soft blue eyes that had conversed so freely a moment before Stella arrived hardened and I was faced with those intimidating icy depths. Something in him had shifted. Maybe I had just imagined it before, but I could have sworn something had changed. His demeanor resumed its normal condescending manner. Whomever it was that I had been comfortable with, was gone and back was the killer I feared.

The guestroom? What's wrong with the guest room? Oh.

I could tell by the look of controlled anger on his face, the last thing Sylas wanted was for Stella to stay in there. He didn't want her to go in the room where I had been held captive. The room where he had taken someone's life.

"I'm in the process of renovating it and it's not quite suitable for annoying siblings just yet so I'll stay there while you get to stay in my luxurious master bedroom," he bargained.

"Okay, but you better not be cranky when you wake up."

"You said you'd be gone early. Hopefully, you will be out of here before I even wake up," His tone made it sound as if he was joking, but I could tell he was serious. He didn't want to risk having her around any longer than necessary.

Stella raised her slender hands up in surrender, "Alright. I get it. I won't overstay my welcome," she paused and looked at me. Now that she was on my left side she had a good view of my injured face, "Whoa. That's a bit of a mark you've got there."

I covered the sutured area with a cupped palm self-consciously, "Yeah I

had a bit of an accident." "Obviously."

Sylas visibly tensed. He cleared his throat, "You know, Stella, it's not polite to talk to others that way."

She moved her hands from around her and raised them in frustration, "Where are your pillows?"

"Somewhere that you can't find them and use as projectiles," he laughed as his anger dissipated.

The rest of the day passed by quickly. The snow eventually stopped and as predicted, a few inches of ice was left on the ground. I did my best to act in the least conspicuous way possible. Sylas didn't want his secrets outed and I didn't want my family at risk. While he may have been concerned about Stella finding out about who he really was, he didn't mind her presence as much as he joked he did. It was so strange to see them interact. As I watched them tease and toy with one another, I was taken aback by the normalcy of it all. Seeing the siblings together reminded me that besides being just a killer, he was human. The younger, female version of him only solidified that belief. The two of them were connected in a way only a lifetime together could foster. Spending their childhoods together meant they knew each other's mannerisms very well and it made for some interesting jokes and conversations.

Throughout all this, I remained in the background. I observed, but rarely participated and left them to banter and play. Despite what Sylas had told me about how his sister grew up and his defensiveness for her faded, I didn't believe that was the full truth. He said he would be able to kill her but chose, out of convenience, not to. I didn't think he realized how wrong he was. While he thought he was capable of killing anything that didn't register as his strange version of innocent, his sister was another exception. He might not be able to love, but he certainly held some affection for his sister and that bond would stop him from harming her.

"I'm starved. Do you have any actual food?" Stella asked as

she headed to the kitchen. Sylas followed her and I slipped behind him.

"Yes, there's plenty of stuff in the fridge. And since you're offering." With her head, inside of the refrigerator Stella answered, "Fine. I'll

make us some dinner. You can't cook for shit anyway. Is Piper staying for dinner?" She closed the fridge and waited for my reply.

"Since I couldn't get rid of you because of the snow, it would be unfair if I made her deal with the icy roads."

"So, a third plate, then?"

"Yes, please," I used my voice for myself. I couldn't let Sylas answer every time.

The roads shouldn't be too bad as we were in a state that was prepared to deal with bad weather, but I didn't bring this up. The meal was a strange assortment of things Stella had put together. Apparently, Sylas didn't have any real food and we had to settle down to a dinner of an edible hodgepodge. Despite that, it was all very tasty.

We were seated alongside the granite topped island. Sylas was in the middle with Stella and me on his adjacent sides. I ate quietly while they discussed trivial things. The evening held a light atmosphere that was soon interrupted by Stella. Although they had been joking, she took the opportunity to slip something more serious into the conversation.

"You ought to come by and visit mom sometime. She told me you hadn't visited in a while. I'm sure a quick visit would make her whole week."

He took another mouthful of food to delay his response. "It's a bit of a drive."

"You're off from work this weekend. The least you could do is spare one afternoon."

"Alright," he agreed unhappily. While Stella couldn't understand, I knew why he was reluctant. When he talked about wanting to kill his father, he said it was because he was the easiest target and since he had excluded his sister that meant his mother could have been a potential target. If he was feeling out of control, he didn't want to risk killing his mother. It, as he had repeated many times, was not out of guilt but social obligation. Killing random people was one thing, but harming family was in a separate category altogether.

He stood up from his seat abruptly. "I think it's about time we prepared for bed."

"Are you kidding me? It's only eight o'clock. That's way to early."

"If you intend to keep your promise of leaving early, then

you might want as much sleep as you can get."

She gave him the finger and walked away, "Okay, bro."

I didn't hide my disgust at the foul gesture and Sylas laughed when he caught sight of my expression. A screamed rent through the air and we froze. Rushing down the hall was a hysterical Stella.

"What happened?" Sylas asked with false concern.

"There's blood!" She was panting hard and talking in-between shallow breaths.

"Where?"

"The guestroom! I went to see what types of renovation you were making so that I could judge you for it, but all I saw was blood! It's smeared all over the carpet," she rambled.

Sylas placed a large hand on her shoulder, "Calm down, it is alright. It's not what you think."

"It's mine," I piped in upon seeing him struggle for an explanation. I pointed to the injury on my face, "That's where this happened." "There was a lot of blood. I mean a lot."

"It was deep enough to require stitches," I offered, "It was pretty big." Sylas nodded, "I didn't have time to clean up the area before you came and I figured it was better to ignore it than try to scare you."

She looked between us suspiciously but made no further comment, "Then where do you plan to sleep?"

"We'll sleep on the couches in the living room."

"We?"

"Piper and I, since there's plenty of room. She'll take the couch and I can have the loveseat."

She still appeared shaken, but was significantly calmer, "Sure. You and this friend that I've never heard of until today are just going to happen to sleep in close proximity," She winked and he removed his hand from her shoulder.

After she was out of earshot Sylas said, "You covered for me." "Did I really have a choice?"

He thought about it for a moment and then answered, "No. It is in both of our best interests that we play along and wait this out." "You need to be careful," I warned.

"I'm always careful."

"But more so this time," I insisted. "Why?"

"Because you happen to be very close with your sister and she was suspicious after seeing that blood. No doubt she sensed something was off right in the beginning. She's probably the only person who really knows you and she *will* figure it out."

"You give her too much credit," he scoffed. "She may know me but, just as I know her, it doesn't mean we really care.

She wouldn't be worried enough to investigate. As you've witnessed, we talk without really revealing anything. We've learned not to bother with each other's lives. Even if she is suspicious, it wouldn't be enough so that she would look into it."

"You're wrong. She actually cares about you. No one just walks into their sibling's house, finds blood, and quickly dismisses it. She knows there's more to the story and you better pray she's gone before she finds out."

He pouted, "I don't need hope. My secrets will remain and you will do nothing to hinder it."

He was facing the other side of the living room, but my position allowed me to see part of the hallway. I squinted as I tried to make out the dark shape barely visible in the distance. Was that a shadow? *It couldn't be Stella, could it? And if it was, is she close enough to hear what he had just said?*

I sighed, "I've come to terms with my place and I know I can't stop you. I am the only thing you needn't worry about."

He pulled his black sweatshirt off and tossed it onto the side of the chair. Underneath, he wore a white tank top which left his broad shoulders exposed. He stretched before sitting down on the loveseat. I took my respective space on the sofa and lay down.

Sylas sank into his seat and said, "I guess it's going to be another long night."

I rolled onto my back and snuggled deeper into the dark leather. "How many more of these am I going to have? Nights, I mean."

"If things go the way I want them to, not many."

I hugged my chest and found comfort in my own embrace. This could be one of my last nights and here I was, close to my would-be-murderer and relaxing, "This whole situation is really messed up."

"Yes," he hummed, "But few things faze me anymore."

"I should be the one saying that. Nothing has ever affected you, but I'm pretty sensitive."

"This is true," he agreed with a laugh. "Seeing you for the first time, though, was a bit of a shock to my system. I never expected it would end up like this."

I turned over to my side so that I could face him. I put my hands together and placed them beneath my face, "You'll still get what you want in the end. It's just been a longer journey, but that's probably what you want."

His chest rose and fell in a hypnotizing rhythm as he relaxed and remained awake, "Why would I want this?"

"Isn't the hunt supposed to be the best part?" I explained with a question of my own.

He shook his head and strands of gold swayed around his angular face, "Not for me. I hate the whole chase. It's tedious. That's why I prefer to take whatever's convenient. The best part comes at the end, so why string it along?"

"A cat that doesn't play with his meal."

His eyes glinted in the dim light. The sun had set and without the added light, the whole house grew darker. He hadn't bothered to turn on any of the light fixtures and allowed the home to bask in the shade.

The sound of footsteps broke our silent communication. The thrumming against the marble floors was too loud to belong to one of the dogs.

Without turning his head Sylas called, "Stell?" "Yeah?" a voice croaked nervously.

Sylas shifted his position after hearing the audible tremor in her voice, "What are you doing?" Leather squeaked as he stood up.

"What do you mean?" She was cloaked by the darkness of the house and Sylas flicked a switch along the wall. Stella shrunk back as soon as the light hit her.

"What's wrong?" he asked with a frown. Something was amiss with his sister and he wanted to know why.

I sat up along the couch to get a better view. Stella had changed into a T-shirt. It was too long on her and it almost reached her knees. She must have gotten it from the bedroom and was barefoot, although her leggings from earlier were still there. She looked to me with a panicked expression before eyeing her brother warily.

"What's going on, Stell?" Sylas repeated quietly. His back was to me, but I could tell from his firm posture and tensed muscles that he was taking this situation very seriously.

"That's not Piper's blood in there, is it?"

"What?" Sylas gasped, taken aback. "Of course, it is. She had an accident."

"Tell me the truth!" she demanded.

"That is the truth."

She walked past her brother and stood before me. I was still seated on the couch so she towered over me, "Is he telling the truth?"

I paused but then confirmed what Sylas had said, "Yes."

Her eyes narrowed at my hesitation. She turned back to her concerned brother, "What are those secrets you're hiding from me, then?"

"I have no idea what you are talking about," his jaw tightened as he clenched his teeth.

"Yes, you do," Stella's voice had gone eerily calm. "I heard you two talking."

"You've misinterpreted what you've heard."

Her hands settled on her hips, "Well, then explain to me what I heard."

I remained on the couch and tried to stay as small as possible to avoid any attention. Sylas' shoulders dropped. "I can't." I witnessed the very articulate man at a lack for words. He couldn't think of something on the spot that would cover whatever she had overheard.

"What do you mean you *can't*?" "Just know, it's not what you think."

"Is this why you've been acting so strange lately. Wait a minute, this all started around the time…" She gasped, "Gravo."

He didn't even deny it. "It's what you wanted," he reasoned, "You cursed that man the day you saw him. You know he's the one who did it."

His confirmation only further stunned Stella. She must have expected him to deny it. "No. you're lying," He shook his head sadly. "SYLAS!" she screamed, "WHAT DID YOU DO?"

"What you wanted," he repeated.

The clap of her palm melded with his face that rang through the house, "Don't you blame this on me. Of course, I wanted justice for dad but not like this! You *killed* him. You *killed* a man."

"Yes," he confirmed.

"And you," she pointed a slender finger at me, "You knew, didn't you?" I nodded with the fear that my voice would fail.

She pulled at the sides of her face hysterically. "Oh my God," she whispered, "The police are out there looking for that man's killer, and here you are!"

Sylas tried to comfort her by placing a hand along her face, but she recoiled from his touch, "I didn't mean to upset you."

"Upset me?" she shrilled, "You did the unthinkable. Who are you? My brother wouldn't do something like that."

"I am your brother," he growled, "I just did what needed to be done." "No, you didn't. You've bloodied your hands. I hated the man, but you shouldn't have ruined yourself over him!"

"I haven't ruined myself," he defended. "I still am who I always have been."

Of course, the person he had always been was a killer, but since Stella didn't need to know that, I stifled my hysterical laugh.

"You haven't ruined yourself? You have his blood in your home!"

"As I've explained, that is Piper's blood from her accident. Yes, I killed him, but that is not his blood. I cut him down in his apartment as I'm sure you've heard the news."

He was trying to explain the blood, but he made a critical mistake. The first man he killed had been in the victim's apartment, but that didn't mean he should have corrected her on that technicality. Had he played it off as Gravo's blood, she wouldn't have looked past the first murder. There was a history between them and his first kill. If that was the only time she thought he would ever do it, there could be a chance to save the quickly dissolving relationship. In his haste to correct her, Sylas' error could destroy everything he had worked for. Stella already didn't believe that the stained carpet was the result of my blood. If she paired that suspicion with what she overheard in the hallway, there was no telling what type of conclusion she could draw.

Stella's eyes widened, "You killed Gravo and that's awful in itself but it's more than that, isn't it? You were just saying how the hunt wasn't as important as the end," she repeated what she had heard while she eavesdropped.

Sylas inhaled and exhaled slowly as he tried to contain himself. Finally, he spoke, "I've always been different. And it would appear you've concluded why."

Stella's face was crestfallen, "No, Sy. It can't be true. Please tell me this is all a joke."

He took a step forward and she took a step back. When he realized she wasn't going to fold, he stomped away. Neither of us made a move as he walked away and into the kitchen. When he returned he held his favorite knife, "It's no joke." His voice had deepened and there was this rasp that left me with goosebumps. It was the voice he used before he killed with some slight variation. It was Cain's voice.

"What does that make you?" Stella asked warily as she took another cautious step back.

"A killer." "And Piper?"

"My hostage," He twirled the blade around his fingers with practiced dexterity. He looked strangely regretful and I knew he wasn't actually going to use the knife tonight. He wasn't going to kill her; he just wanted her to get the message.

"This can't be happening," she panicked. "Why? What happened to you?"

He held his head low and stared at the ground before looking up at her, "Nothing happened." The icy passion in his eyes faded. It was something I had witnessed before. It was as if Cain, which usually slithered so close to the surface, disappeared deep inside him. He was temporarily without Cain, he claimed was a part of him. Instead of a killer threatening his sister, he was a lost boy who didn't know what to do, "I've always been this. It's just recently, I've indulged in my desires."

"You're evil," Stella seethed.

"Yes," with one final word of validation, he severed the bond between the two of them. It was clear by looking at Stella that she had detached herself from him. Where she had been gentle and playful toward her sibling, she now stared coldly at a murderous stranger.

With pulsating anger, Stella charged at him. Sylas made no attempt to move and even dropped his knife as she sped forward. She smashed into him with enough force and knocked him to the ground. The collision was loud and, even having seen it coming, I still jumped.

Stella pushed him to the ground, "HOW MANY PEOPLE HAVE YOU HURT?" She screamed in his face.

"Eight," her fist connected with his jaw as he answered. Sylas grinned, "And I enjoyed every moment of it," he said as he egged her on.

I had no idea why he was tempting her. Maybe he thought she deserved to take her anger out on him or maybe on some masochistic level, he needed her to harm him to make up for what he'd done. There was no point in me getting tangled up between the dueling siblings so I stayed put and watched it all happen from my spot on the couch. Sylas remained motionless as Stella pummeled him with her fists. She was relentless as she continued to slam her knuckles into every inch of his face.

"I loved watching the life drain from their eyes while they bled," he hissed through a gargled voice. He moved his head to the side while she paused as he spit out a wad of blood.

Stella's shoulders jerked up and down rapidly. I could only see part of her face, but it was enough to notice the tears rolling down her cheeks. "I looked up to you as a kid," she sobbed. "Everything was a lie, wasn't it?"

Sylas reached a hand up but she smacked it away, "Yes. My dreams are occupied by deaths I've caused, but they are far from nightmares."

Tears streamed down her face and fell onto his chest. She reached to the side and grabbed the knife he had dropped. She held it shakily.

"Stella, please," Sylas murmured through a mouth full of blood. His face was beginning to swell slightly, and the tan skin along his face reddened.

To his surprise and horror, she angled the blade so that it was not facing him, but her. Sylas heaved upwards upon seeing her intention, managed to dislodge her from himself, and attempted to grab hold of her arm as she stood up.

110

He jumped to his feet as quickly as he could, but it was not fast enough. Stella gained some distance and still had possession of the knife.

She looked at him regretfully, "For the longest time, all I ever wanted was to be just like my big brother. You were my friend when no one else was. You were all I had," she confessed.

Sylas lunged forward but in the split second it took him to reach her,

Stella had already plunged the knife into her chest, "NO!" he roared.

The blade was lodged in her thorax just to the left of her sternum. It was a lethal blow. "Sorry," she wheezed, "But I'd rather not give you the honor of killing me."

Sylas scooped her up in his arms, "No. No. No. I wouldn't have ever killed you. I couldn't," the reality of it hit him. Despite what he had always thought, he finally realized that, just as he was unable to kill me, he couldn't have murdered his sibling.

I stood up and ran over to where they were positioned. Then, as I came within a few feet from the duo, I saw something I never imagined I would see.

The evil creature I had considered dammed and incapable of feeling any real emotion fell apart. As Stella's breathing slowed and evened out, Sylas broke. As he held his baby sister during her final moments, he cried. The low, distressed wail he let out was heartbreaking. I turned away from the intimate moment.

The demon had found his heart. Unfortunately, it came at the price of the one person he might have actually loved.

Chapter 13

It was a surreal feeling. *Is this grief?* As the body in my arms grew limp, I mourned her lost spirit. My gut twisted painfully as I was overcome with emotion. Where was Cain? He usually blocked me from feeling of pain and without him, I could barely cope. I needed something to stop this foreign sensation.

"Stella," I whispered hopefully. I knew she was gone, but I had to hear her one last time. She had been my only true friend. And even though it took me so long to realize, she was the one who kept me grounded. She was what had stopped me from killing as a child and it was only when I was away from her that Cain had become so uncontrollable.

When I looked down, the blue eyes, like my own, were directed at me. She stared at me with glossy eyes that no longer saw. I shifted her weight in my arms so that I could reach around with my hand and shut her eyes. It was wrong to see her this way. She should be walking around, irritating me like she always did. But that was something she would never do again.

For the first time in my life, I felt wetness pooled around my eyes. Soon the tears flowed down my face freely. It was my turn to return the gesture as my symbols of sadness fell onto her chest. The tears I shed were genuine, and it was the only time in my short life that I had felt true despair.

Blood seeped through her T-shirt and continued to flow even after she had passed. Holding her so close meant that the scarlet essence of her life also stained my clothes. I didn't care though. This blood was the only reminder of what had once been.

When I looked up from my sorrow, I saw her. Piper. She was turned away in what I assumed was her way of giving me privacy.

As I looked between the two women I could never kill, another realization slammed into me. I did not really view Piper as a dog. While she did have similar traits to my mutts; there was something I had been unable to identify. Until now. The reason I had been so drawn to her was because she was Stella. She was not necessarily my sister in the way she acted or thought, but for how she was. She was the embodiment of what I considered untouchable. I had spent my whole childhood watching over Stella and drilling it into my head that she was good and should never become one of my victims.

That philosophy had carried over to Piper. Of course, the way I felt about Piper was an attraction far beyond that of a sibling.

As I hugged the remnants of what was once my sister, I continued to glance in Piper's direction. She still had yet to turn around and for that, I was grateful. My emotional state was pathetic and I didn't want anyone to witness me as I broke on the inside.

It would appear that in the battle of wills, I had lost. I had found my breaking point, but I had yet to discover Piper's. And I needed to find it out quickly. I would still kill her as I had promised, especially now after everything that had happened.

Piper was a living reminder of what I had lost and I could not have that horrible cloud hanging over my head forever. I would have to return to normal eventually and Piper was the only remaining person that could draw such a reaction from me. I would worry about that later. For the moment, all I wanted to do was stay where I was as I let out my trapped feelings. I cried a laughable amount, but I stifled my sniffles so Piper wouldn't hear my sobs.

"I am a monster," I whispered into Stella's hair. "And that will never change, but know your death will not be forgotten. I truly cared about you, Stell," my voice shook pathetically as regret laced my words.

After I was done expressing my grief, I placed her rapidly cooling body on the floor. I pulled the knife from between her ribs and placed it beside her. I moved her arms to rest peacefully at her sides. When rigor mortis set in, I wanted her to maintain a dignified pose. She deserved that much at least.

"You didn't kill her," Piper stated bluntly. There was nothing soothing about her words, nor was it meant to be.

"I wish I had," the last thing I had expected her to do was take her own life. If she really wanted to die because of me, I should have done it myself. Instead, I had to watch her take action and not be able to do anything about it. If I had killed her it would have still been awful, but I would have had some control. I hated being helpless.

"You wouldn't have been able to go through with it," Piper returned. "But it would have been *my* decision. Not hers."

"And that's what she wanted. She wanted it to be her decision. She thought you would do it so she chose to do it herself and take that option away from you."

"She hated what I was," I couldn't blame her though. She had every right to despise me.

"Which is why she separated herself from you."

"Permanently," I specified. "Death cannot be undone. She's gone forever," I emphasized the last word. She would never return.

Piper looked at Stella's body and sighed, "She was a good person. She's in a better place now."

I didn't even dispute the plausibility of it. "But I'm not good." "No, you're not," Piper confirmed.

"So, in death."

"You won't be reunited."

"Because while she's in Heaven, I belong in Hell," my voice was grated. Even if something better really existed, I wouldn't be a part of it. Our separation was eternal; no matter what.

I had tainted something so precious that she felt the need to kill herself before she could be overcome by Cain. I had brought death to the only human that had ever cared for me. While Piper had similar traits, we met under unpleasant circumstances and she only knew me as the monster I was. Stella, at least, had years to bond with my false self. Piper had never seen me with such a façade, and it was pointless to try such tactics now. She had seen me at my worst and there was no turning back. Until I finally killed her, she would only know me as a cruel being that enjoyed destroying life.

"I can't bury her with all of the snow. I'll have to wait until it melts and dig her a proper grave," I reasoned out loud. Piper remained silent, "I could always put her outside regardless to help preserve her body, but I'd be afraid the dogs would be interested in her," I moaned. "I just hate to wait too long and there's nowhere to keep her."

"Burn her," Piper suggested with a voice much darker than her own. Surprise, aside from her strange attitude, it was a viable idea. I nodded,

"That's not a bad idea."

After some thought, I went to work. I put on a large jacket, sneakers, and beanie. I also grabbed a flashlight and shovel before heading out into the frosty night. I trudged through the sea of ice with only the small pocket of illumination from my flashlight, until I found a small clearing. It had a radius of at least twenty feet and would be a good spot. I marched into the center and used the back of the shovel to sweep away the snow. I stopped when I had an area several square feet in size. It would be plenty of room for her body while making sure there was still enough space between the body and the fire. Satisfied with my work, I headed to the house and grabbed additional supplies along with her body.

"Is it ready?" Piper greeted my return with a question.

I nodded and bent down and picked up what had once been my sister. Her body had already begun to grow stiff in the time it took for the preparations. Piper obediently grabbed the tank of gasoline I had taken from the garage and some other flammable items. She now wore one of my large hoodies to fight against the cold as we stepped outside.

I didn't even need the flashlight, but I still used it for Piper's sake. I knew the spot well and, as I suspect, I would continue to know it. I could have found my way through the dark on feel alone, but it was much faster with the small light source.

I still couldn't believe the unmoving form in my arms was Stella. It had all played out like an unrealistic nightmare. Hours ago, she had been lively and full of spunk, but now was another corpse. In life she had been beautiful, but death haunted her features and dulled her radiant shimmer.

I halted when we reached our destination. Piper noticed the spot I had cleared away and hurried over. She spread the materials along the cold, barren ground, before coating it all with gasoline. She had been very helpful with all this and seemed oddly comfortable with it all, even though it involved so much death. Maybe Stella's death had affected her too, saw her own future through Stella's dead eyes, and had accepted it.

With the space covered and prepped, I walked over and slowly lowered my load onto the ground. I placed a hand on her cold cheek and whispered, "Goodbye."

Piper started to lift the gas can to hose down the body, but I stopped her and took it for myself. I doused my sister in the chemical fluid until the can ran dry. I went to wipe my hands in the nearby snow before I fetched a lighter from my pocket. Piper stepped to the edge of the clearing as I lowered the small flame to the pile. It took a moment for it to catch fire. When it finally lit, the flames grew immediately. I stepped back and watched the progression of the orange element as it grew in size and swallowed its offering. I had chosen a spot to observe Stella's top half. I wanted to see her face the entire time. Soon enough, the flames engulfed her head. I didn't once look away as her face slowly burned and shriveled into blackness.

I could have walked away at any time and left the fire to do its work, but I refused to leave. I would witness it all. I had been there since she began and I would watch it end. I had welcomed my sister into the world and now I forced her out of it. I may have been young at the time, but I remembered her birth in great detail. I remembered holding the small bundle and being told she was my sister. We were tied by blood and I had watched in fascination as the tiny baby opened its eyes. I couldn't describe the protectiveness I, at four years old, felt for the tiny human when I saw my own blue irises reflected on her face. As much as she managed to annoy me, I had never held any ill thoughts against her. She was special. And now, the last evidence of her entire existence burned away into nothingness.

It took hours. The process was by no means fast and with the wind blowing hard, I had to relight the half-burned corpse several times. It was unlike anything else I had ever seen. Watching her flesh contort and bake was something I had never and would never see again. The smell of the roasted body was grotesque and my stomach flipped several times when it was at its strongest, but I never looked away. Piper had returned to the house when she realized I wasn't going to budge until it was done. My stare never wavered. The only rest my eyes received from the sight was when I blinked.

As the flames began to diminish for the final time, I made no attempt to reignite them. The skeletal face before me was enough proof that it was complete. I waited until the final spark died before I turned away from the grizzly sight. I would still have to bury the bones, but they didn't require preparation. I kicked some snow on top of the remains to hide it from the dogs before leaving. I walked slowly to the house, noting that my toes and hands were completely numb. The sun had partially risen and the sky was a bright orange as the night faded away.

I entered through the back door and kicked my shoes off and shed my large jacket. Piper was fast asleep on the couch and I left her to rest peacefully. I headed to my own bedroom and sunk under the covers of my bed. My muscles ached from standing in one position all night long. I reached under the pillow to bring it forward and my hand touched something solid. I pushed away my tiredness temporarily to investigate. I pulled out a phone. It was an older iPhone model and I wondered who's it was for a moment before I remembered that Stella was supposed to have stayed here last night. I turned the device on, but it asked for a passcode. I entered one, two, three, four and sure enough the device unlocked. I let out a small laugh at the predictability of her actions. I browsed through the phone without any reservations. I didn't care if it was disrespectful to search through a dead person's belongings. The phone was once my sister's and if I wanted to look through it as a reminder of how she lived, so be it.

Aside from all of the games, there was little left behind on the phone. The only social media app she had was for Facebook and she hadn't even finished registering her account. *I know she wasn't very social but still–she did have some friends...Right?*

Looking through her call records I noticed that my name was the only one that showed up. When I went through her messages it was a similar thing. She had talked to a few other people, at least, but all of her texts to them were short and professional. Nothing like the annoying ones she always sent to me. I hadn't turned on my phone since yesterday morning and I remembered her telling me that she had texted before coming over. Since I had never bothered to look at what she sent, I decided to view those messages now.

Hey!

Are you there? Sylas?

I'm headed your way. See you soon ;p

I had not responded to any of her messages. I had ignored one of our last conversations. Had I seen the text that she was coming over, I could have prepared better. I might have even been able to stop her from learning what she did. Had I listened to her, I might have been able to prevent her death.

My chest tightened. Regret oozed from my entire being. I could have had her happy and alive by my side instead of a pile of bones in a forest. All it would have taken to change everything was seeing one little text. My regret morphed into anger and I chucked the phone across the room. It hit the wall and shattered on impact. I wanted to scream until my lungs felt raw. One message. Just *one* message had altered the course of everything. I jumped off the bed and exited the room. I slammed the door so forcibly that I might have broken the hinges, but I didn't care one bit.

I tried to march past the living room, but Piper rose from the couch and stopped me, "What are you doing?" she asked, "You are scaring the dogs!" Behind her all four dogs shrunk away.

I growled as ferociously as possible. I was trying to sound as animalistic as I could, and it worked. All of the canines, including Piper, jumped in response. I instantly regretted it when I saw the fear on all five of their faces. I scrubbed my face in my hands and apologized.

I walked around Piper and to the spot where I had removed the knife from Stella last night. "I found Stella's phone," I explained, "and then I crushed it."

Piper watched me closely. There was no emotion on her face. She was a statue.

I didn't expect her to comfort me, given the fact that she was still technically my captive, but any soothing words would have been helpful. I was in an emotional turmoil and I couldn't handle it.

I have always had a high pain tolerance, but this was a different type of suffering. It was emotional. The worst type of pain is the kind that doesn't leave a mark. A wound justified any temporary weakness and was visible for the world to see. Psychological struggles were hidden and made no obvious excuse for the behavior that complimented it. Unbroken skin is quickly forgotten, but stars measure a lifetime.

I grabbed the knife off the ground and did the only thing I

could think of to make myself feel better. The metal blade dug into the skin along my right cheek. I didn't wince at the sharp pinch, but relaxed instead. The only way I could handle this emotional distress was to find a way to manifest the pain. Something to redirect the pain to.

Piper watched me quietly and made no move to stop me. Maybe she hoped I was going for more than a simple cut on my face. That would at least free her from this terrible place, but I made no such move to do anything further than the gash near my mouth. I looked into Piper's tired face and smiled when I spotted her own scar. It had been unintentional, but our cuts mirrored one another.

"Hoping I would follow in Stella's footsteps?" I asked her jokingly, but I did really want to hear her answer.

She pushed a lock of her dark hair behind her ear. "I've stopped hoping to escape from here. The only thing I pray for now is fair judgment in the end." She had not abandoned her beliefs in the end, but did doubt that they would save her from this predicament.

"You've given up."

She didn't deny my statement. "I have to think about the bigger picture now. There's nowhere for me to go. I'm just as trapped as you are."

"I'm not trapped," I defended. She didn't argue further.

"Sylas?"

It was the first time she had addressed me by my own name. "What?"

"You didn't smile."

I didn't get the connection, "I didn't smile?" "You didn't smile for Stella as she died."

Her observation should have stirred up the unpredictable emotions that had been surfacing all day, but I didn't feel anything. Being so close to her seemed to dull the effects of grief, "No, I didn't."

"Why? She was much more important to you than I am."

I swiped the blood that dripped down my chin. I had cut it nearly as deep as Piper's and I probably needed stitches, "I wouldn't necessarily say that. You two may be alike in some ways, but you are ultimately different people."

"But she cared so much about you."

"It's a mercy I can only grant once and I've already reserved that for you," Stella might have been the person closest to me, but that didn't mean I didn't want someone else to be closer.

"I'm only a hostage. If I hadn't witnessed your first kill, I wouldn't even be here. Whereas Stella was your sister."

"And our relationship was one built off the unconditional

118

love families are supposed to have. It was circumstantial. Had it not been for that connection, we would have been strangers."

"But you weren't just strangers."

"We could have been and if that were the case, I would have killed her easily and not felt anything. Familial bonds make it easy to care about your kin, but that's a simple thing. The types of relationships formed between people who have no obligation to care for one another are far more impressive. They show a true connection and that is not an easy thing to forge."

She shook her head, "I will never understand the way you think."

I laughed, "The same can be said about you. We're very opposite from one another."

Her lips quirked upwards and I found myself smiling with her. I was

actually relieved to see her smile. It warmed some part inside me that had long been frozen. My feelings about Stella's death were overpowered by Piper. Not only did she have the power to suppress Cain, but she also rid me of my pain. If it was anybody else, I would find some way to keep them close, but we were in a very different situation. She wasn't some stranger I could convince to spend the night. She was supposed to be my next victim and prolonging the inevitable was only draining on the both of us. I would have to get rid of her soon for her presence was slowly becoming consuming. I couldn't get addicted to something I was going to get rid of.

That night as I tossed fitfully in my sleep, I was overrun by a memory I thought had disappeared.

"Sylaaaaasss," a shrill voice yelled playfully. I looked up in time to see the small form darting toward me.

I groaned as the young girl wrapped her arms tightly around my chest, "What is it?" I asked in a staged way. It was all I could do, not to sigh regretfully at the young girl's intrusion. I pretended to be as excited as she was to avoid hurting her feelings.

Stella lifted her head and smiled widely. Her grin large enough to reveal the gaps in her mouth where her adult teeth had yet grown in to replace their fallen counterparts, "You have to see what I bought today. Mom helped me pick out some fun stuff!" Her head bobbled around with each word and the sloppy pigtails slapped blonde hair across her face. Her fair complexion was marred with a light sprinkling of freckles across her cheeks.

I pinched the bridge of her nose and she giggled. Her bubbly laugh stopped when I spoke again, "Cool! I can't wait to see it all. Are you excited for school?"

Her lips turned down into a pout, "The shopping was fun

but I don't wanna go to school."

I laughed and ruffled the frizzy, blonde hair on her head, "Come on, it's not so bad. First grade is really easy and you'll like it. I promise the spelling tests aren't as bad as you've heard," I consoled optimistically.

She shifted her feet nervously, "I'm not worried about tests. I'm just scared about new people. I won't have any friends," her lip started to tremble. If I didn't act quickly, she would be in tears soon.

Despite being so young, I was already tall enough to tower over Stella. Granted, there was an age gap and she had a good height for her age, but I felt like a giant next to the lithe girl. "Friends are easy to make," I promised. Not having many social connections, myself; everything I said was false, but I didn't have much choice. I didn't feel like dealing with a crying sister, so I tried to diffuse the situation the best way I could.

"Really?" Her face lightened slightly, but she was still on the verge of tears.

"Yeah," I confirmed. "And no matter what—you have me."

"I do? You're gonna be my friend?" Her blue eyes widened.

Because what ten-year-old bout didn't want to hang out with his little sister? I kept that sarcastic thought to myself and just nodded. "Sure."

Stella squealed excitedly. She clapped her hands together before she remembered her initial excitement. "Oh, I still wanna show you what I got!"

I went along with everything and ogled at the sparkly pencils and bright blue backpack she had gotten. She rambled on and I nodded with mild interest. She was so easily excitable. That, paired with her innocence, made her seem like a puppy.

I woke up gasping. The T-shirt I had worn to bed clung to my frame as a sheen of sweat oozed from my pores. I was breathing shakily as I recounted what had just happened in my head. My stomach twisted at the thought. What a cruel way my mind continued to remind me of my mistakes. I had destroyed something, I had once deemed so perfect and there was no way to fix it.

My mind automatically shifted to Piper. While I had originally hoped to eliminate every part of her that made her different, I now cringed at the idea. The destruction of her perfection was not something I think I could handle.

My perspective must have changed drastically as I went from feeling excited about killing her to nearly becoming ill. My mind and body were locked in an endless struggle and not even I could predict the outcome.

Chapter 14

The days dragged by slowly with each hour that ticked by slower than the last. Time was limited as I opted to remain in this cage and contemplated my very existence. When I was gone, would anything I had worked to achieve still matter? Would all my accomplishments fall without me? Would I even be missed? I thought back to my family and friends and knew that I would, but how long would it take for them to realize what happened? The last they had seen me, I was climbing into a car with what they probably assumed was my boyfriend. Would they await my return only to oust me when they thought I had abandoned them?

There were too many variables to consider and I forced myself to focus on something else. There was no point pondering over the 'what ifs.' There was also no need for me to be stressed out. I could tell my death was nearing. Sylas had slowly detached himself from me and hadn't seen him in hours. I was locked in the bathroom in hopes of some privacy, but I had no idea where he was.

The snow had melted two days ago and Sylas had been sure to bury the bones the moment the ground changed from ice to mud. I knew the death of his sister had been hard for him and had never seen him so distressed when she killed herself. A crack had formed inside him, but when he had returned from disposing Stella's remains; the look on his face told me he had broken. Only a single thread of morality remained. Once that was gone, he was bound to snap. There would be nothing left stopping him from harming me or the dogs. While it would have been unthinkable before, he was growing more and more unpredictable, and he started to look at his dogs with disgust instead of the affection that I had seen previously. He still took care of them, but the enthusiasm was gone and the dread of responsibility showed.

I looked over myself in the mirror. I had tied my hair back into a tight bun and soothed any small bumps with my hands systematically. Since I didn't have many clothing options, I was forced to raid Sylas' closet. Aside from a few pairs of casual clothing, the man owned a lot of suits. They all looked and felt expensive; I was impressed. He obviously had lots of money, but I assumed it had been inherited. If the formal clothing was any indication, he had an important job with a large pay grade. I had chosen to wear one of his large hoodies and a pair of baggy sweatpants. I drew a line at underwear, though.

I had full access of the house and I gladly utilized the showers. I looked in the mirror as I scrutinized my appearance. While the clothes I wore were clean, I felt dirty. I despised having to wear my captor's clothes. They held his masculine scent and I hated it. Every time I took a deep breath, it was a forcible reminder that I was no longer in control of my own life. I would be at his mercy until the moment he decided I should die.

There was a knock at the bathroom door and I jumped. It was the spare bathroom and I figured he wouldn't disrupt me as everything he needed was in the master bathroom.

"Piper, are you in there?" a voice I had grown very familiar with, asked.

"Yes."

"Are you almost done?"

"Yes," the single word of agreement had become one of the only phrases I had used. I waited a few moments but no footsteps sounded to signal his retreat and I could still see his shadow through the bottom of the door. He wasn't going to leave anytime soon.

Knowing he wouldn't go away on his own, I glanced in the mirror one last time before I opened the door, "What is it?"

His face was more rugged than usual. He hadn't shaved since recapturing me and he now sported a short beard. It worked well. He had also given up on making his hair conform to a slick shape. Fringes of his bright blond hair dangled in and around his face. He looked scruffy, but not in an unattractive way. If anything, his hair had the asymmetrical laid-back styling that was fashionable. Had someone seen him like this they would have never guessed the stress and grief he had gone through and would assume that it was what he intended. Having seen him formally cleaned up and slick, though, it was easy to see where he had neglected himself.

"I made lunch," he offered. He was wearing a red T-shirt and athletic shorts. At this time of year, it would have been cold to wear something like that, but he kept the house at a cozy temperature.

"You made lunch?"

He shrugged, "I was bored. Are you hungry?"

I was, in fact, very hungry but I was hesitant to trust his gesture. He stared at me intently and while the sky-blue irises had noticeably lost the intensity they once held, it was still intimidating. Finally, I gave in and nodded. He turned around and I followed him as he led me into the kitchen.

I sat down at the island to find a plate with grilled cheese and fruit, "Is this your way of telling me something?"

"What do you mean?"

I poked at the sandwich before taking a small bite, "Is this my last meal?"

He didn't blink and held eye contact for a scary amount of time. "It's Sunday," he commented.

I took a larger bite of my lunch. For someone who couldn't cook he sure made a mean grilled cheese. "And why is that significant?" I asked in-between bites.

"Too much time has already passed."

"So? Are you missing a deadline or something?"

"Not in the literal sense, but yes, something is running out of time." "You mean me," I said without hesitation. I was scared about what

would happen, but I also knew how unlikely it was that I would escape all this alive. I had had many days to think about it and, while it still frightened me, I didn't avoid conversing about it. It was a very possible outcome that I would be dead within the next week and beside Stella in a grave of my own.

"I mean both of us." "Both?" I questioned.

He leaned in close and I stopped eating, "I corrupt you but you still manage to play with my mind." His minty breath blew in my face as he spoke.

"You're buying time," I concluded. "What?"

"I change the way you think and I believe that some part of you deep down likes that."

"There is nothing I like about you taking all the fun away from killing," he defended.

"Then why haven't you killed me yet? I've noticed a change in you. You don't really care about your dogs the way you used to. I see no reason why you would keep me around when you could easily dispose of me like one of your pets, yet here I am."

"Maybe it is for the thrill of making you wait."

"You don't care about the chase. It's all about what happens in the end, right?" I threw the words he had once used back in his face.

He retracted his body and turned around and kicked one of the low cabinets. The small wooden door fell right off its hinges, "The end of you is all I seek," he hissed.

"So, what are you waiting for? Do you want me to love you like Stella did so that way when I die, you will cherish it more?" Prodding the beast was not one of my smartest moves but if I was to go down, I would at least take the knowledge that I sought to my grave.

He grabbed my plate and threw it at me. Having seen what he planned to do, I managed to duck in time and the porcelain plate shattered against the wall. The remainder of my meal laid smooshed amongst the debris of the broken plate. I thought the plate would have been enough to satisfy his anger, but I was wrong. His rampage continued as he rounded the corner and reached the stool I was sitting on. He grabbed my shirt and pulled at the necklace I never took off. With one hard tug, it snapped apart.

"Hey!" I protested.

He dangled the broken chain in front of my face, but moved it away before I could snatch it back, "Do you wish to aggravate me?"

"Do you wish to keep me here forever?"

"Maybe," he admitted quietly, "But that is impossible."

"You wouldn't like keeping me forever," I debated, "The extra time together will not result in what you think it will. Stockholm syndrome is not something that will ever occur. No matter what happens, I will never forgive you."

"I'm not after your love or hate," he fiddled with my necklace. "Then what do you want?"

"To explore my humanity," he rubbed the small golden cross between his fingers, "You seem to have so much influence on me. When I'm in your presence, Cain is nowhere to be found."

"How does that affect your view toward me? I thought you loved being evil," I thought on everything he had told me when he had first captured me.

"I do. Cain allows me to feel great pleasure when I succumb to him, but he's all I've ever known. Maybe I just want to see what I can do without him. Maybe then, I can find real happiness," his confession was honest and I could tell by the rasp in his words how much the admittance cost him. "But if I don't get rid of you soon, I'll never be able to do it. I'll become too attached," his frown was deep as he recounted this revelation.

"So, it's me versus Cain," my heart raced at the potential this offered. I had already accepted I would die at his hands, but this possibility gave me a chance, "How do I win?"

He shook his head. "I don't choose. Cain is all consuming," he paused to hand the necklace back to me, "But so are you." I grabbed the special accessory tightly. It was very precious to me and I was glad he gave it back.

Suddenly, a calloused hand gripped my neck tightly. I gasped desperately and clawed at my throat, "It's anyone's game," he whispered into my ear before he pulled away and disappeared to a different part of the house. I coughed and rubbed at the spot where his fingers had been tightly clasped. I stood up and left the messy kitchen.

Sylas didn't show up for the rest of the day. He was brooding in his room, and I enjoyed my freedom. I went for a walk outside and was met with no protest. The air was frigid, but I hadn't cared. If anything, the cold wind helped to reawaken my senses. The dogs came to greet me and followed me along my stroll. I made sure to avoid the area where Stella had been burned. The last thing I needed was to relive that horror. Despite the clearing smog, the air was still permeated with death. I shuddered at the dreadful atmosphere.

When I returned to the house, I found Sylas sitting on the couch. He was facing the back door I had just come through, but his head was lowered and failed to acknowledge my arrival. When I tried to walk past him, though, he made sure to stop my advance. "Wait," he pleaded.

I stopped and took a seat next to him. *Maybe I am just an obedient dog.*

"What do you need from me?" "I want to talk."

"About what?"

"Anything. Everything. Hell, it doesn't matter."

I had grown so accustomed to his filthy language that I let that slide. Instead, I focused on the other words he said, "You just want to talk?" I paused in disbelief.

He nodded eagerly, "What were you up to outside?" There was no accusation in his voice. He truly only wanted details.

"I just went for a stroll. The dogs joined me too."

He smiled sadly, "Yeah, they love it when someone plays with them outside. The property is perfect for them since they can play and run all they want, but they still prefer human company. I'm glad you gave them some attention. I've neglected them a bit lately," his minor confession was uncalled for and I wondered where this depressing talk could be going. Instead of stalling it, though, I chose to continue with my account.

"I avoided the area where the fire was, though. I didn't want to come across, you know," I added.

"That's understandable. But that's not the area where I buried what was left of her."

"Really? I didn't see any markings anywhere else."

"That's because there are none," he was being straightforward, but firm. "You didn't give her a gravestone?" I asked. After everything, I assumed he would have made a big memorial for Stella. "No. A gravestone isn't necessary."

Not necessary? "But she's not another victim. Don't you want to be able to easily find where your sister rests?"

"No. I don't want anyone finding her. When I allow my

wrongdoings to be discovered, I want her to remain a secret. That's why her location is hidden. She will rest in peace here. It's the closest I will ever be to her again."

Allow his wrongdoings to be discovered? "But no one is going to come here looking for her."

"Oh, but they will." He swallowed as he choked up, "Now keep talking."

"I don't have much else to say," I said slowly growing more and more confused and, as much as I wanted to press him about everything, I knew that in time he would reveal it himself.

"Just do it."

"Why? You could always try talking to me instead of vice versa."

"I need to hear your voice so that I can make sure I made the right decision," His hands trembled as they reached out toward my cheek.

I didn't move as his hands gently caressed me, "What decision?"

"I just turned my confession into the police. I gave them all they should need. Locations, bodies, weapons, and anything else incriminating. Once they verify it, all of the charges against you should be dropped."

"What?" He sounded serious but he had to be joking, "You turned yourself in? What does that even mean? Are you serious?" It was almost too good to be true.

"I'm deadly serious," he confirmed with a pierced tone. He rubbed the cut along my cheek tenderly with a sad smile.

I shook my head expecting this to be anything but reality, "B-but—"

"You've won," he swallowed undecidedly. His voice was knotted and his eyes held an immeasurable expression of sorrow. The blue eyes I had become so familiar with sparkled briefly before they dulled. The fierce passion in his icy gaze was lost and I myself was caught up in his defeat. I had watched the formation of this monster and now I would be the one to see it leave in the wake of its own destruction.

I shook my head, "There is no winner."

"There will be," he corrected. His condescending tone had been scraped down to a whisper. Its impact was different, but still existent. He waved his arms around the room, "I've worked so hard for everything that it seems such a waste, but its best this way," he said that seemingly like a monologue.

I was still in such disbelief that, had it not been for his distressed state, I wouldn't have taken him seriously. It seemed too good to be true. What evil mastermind would just drop everything and turn himself in?

"You're going to prison?" I didn't know if it was some way to make up for all his sins, but no attempt could ever excuse what he had done. It was still better than having him running rampant through the streets, but nothing could repay the lives he had taken.

He let out a hollow laugh, "No, I'm not going to prison."

"But you confessed to the police. You weren't joking about that, right?" His hands fell into his pockets, "Yes. I made sure to get any suspicions off you, but I'm not going to jail."

I scrunched my eyebrows, "I don't understand. Are you going on the run or something?"

"No, of course not. The confession was for you. As for me–I have other plans."

His responses did not help to clarify the situation. From my understanding, he had confessed his crime to get me off the hook—which, I still had no clue as to why he'd done such a thing—but I had no idea where he was going in terms of how he planned to handle it all. There weren't any other options outside of prison time or running away. And, since he stated he planned to participate in neither of those options, I was confused as to what he planned.

"I'm a monster."

"As we've concluded before," I answered. "And I love it."

"Again, discussed before."

"But," he began. "As intoxicating as Cain is, he is also dangerous."

I nodded, "You kill people. Consequences are to be expected."

He shook his head, "I don't mean dangerous in the traditional sense. I'm not worried about the physical consequences our laws could bring. I'm talking about a much worse scenario. This has always been a part of me but, until recently, only a small part. Cain had been there forever, but he's outgrown their small crevice. He is all consuming. Normally I wouldn't care, but you've shown me there's more to it. I can't allow him to pollute me any further, despite my love for him."

"What does stopping this Cain entail?" I probed.

His lips twitched weakly, "I'm taking Stella's advice." "I don't think I get what you're saying."

"She killed herself so I or, rather, Cain couldn't do so. She wanted to have control over her final moments. Control, I've always deeply valued and it seems appropriate that I follow in her footsteps."

Chapter 15

Her look of confusion was priceless. She didn't believe I was doing this for her. Of course, it wasn't really all for her. It was for me too. The longer we were together, the more we corrupted one another. I could never completely give up who I was and it was having a negative impact on Piper. The cheery idealistic woman was replaced by an emotionless shell of her former self. It was a volatile relationship. While I was so consumed by her the last thing I wanted was to end it, but I needed to stop it. It would only continue to bring pain.

There is no redemption for evil. No sacrifice would ever eliminate the dark scars left behind. If I was a demon, then she was an angel. These polar opposites could not coexist. They thrived to eliminate one another. In the end, there would only be destruction.

My actions were not to save her, but to stop myself from seeing what I would become. One thing had become clear in the time we had spent together; neither of us deserved the other. She was too good for me and I was too evil for her. While our connection was undeniable, it had not stemmed from a good place. We were tied together by death and she didn't deserve to lose her angelic qualities, so that I could continue on my selfish path.

There was no place for me in this reality and I didn't want to be a constant reminder of that failure. I was always meant to be a monster; an outcast by Cain. I would never be a hero and my final moments would confirm my cowardice.

"Smile," I instructed her hysterically. My voice was barely above a whisper, but I could tell she heard me by the way her eyebrows rose in confusion.

"Why?" she asked cautiously.

My decision had been made, but I still had a hard time believing in my choice. A laugh escaped my lips before I answered her question, "Because I want the last face I see to be a happy one."

I brought the knife that I had concealed at my side up to my neck. With a sweeping slash, I buried the blade in my flesh deep enough to sever my final connection to life. I dropped my arms, and it took every ounce of restraint not to stem the flow of blood with my hands. A sickening numbness encapsulated my body. Nausea twanged as my scarlet essence spluttered from my busted arteries with an intense force. Dizzy and hanging on to the last blip of consciousness, I looked to Piper. I watched for a smile that never came. My lips twitched in an attempt to tell her to look less grim, but I choked on a mouthful of salty red liquid instead. All I wanted was to leave this world with a joyful expression, but that was not the case. To my utter devastation, she grimaced in shock.

A look of horror was imprinted in my memory as the world went black for that final time.

Epilogue

A warm breeze ruffled my hair. The dark brown wisps swirled around my head at the touch of the wind. The afternoon was pleasant, and I found myself basking in the sunny weather.

I touched a finger to the prominent scar on my face. Over the years it had faded, unlike the memories that came with it. The pink line that marred my left cheek was a constant reminder of what I had gone through, and I shuddered. I had never been the same since I had returned from that demon's house. I was still very religious and firm in my morals, but I no longer had the optimistic attitude of my former self. My naivety had died the moment I met him.

Sylas. That's a name I haven't thought of in a while.

He had been right all along. Death was the only escape, and his had liberated me from his evil presence. After the police reviewed the confession he had called in and examined the evidence in his home, I was freed from suspicion. When I had returned home after that long struggle, there had been a lot of readjustments. Everyone had made a big fuss and had been careful around me, but eventually things returned to normal. I was able to continue on with my life.

A bark interrupted my thoughts, and I looked down at the furry face beside me. Daisy squirmed in place, but didn't tug on the long leash. I had paused in the middle of the sidewalk, and when I continued to move again four fluffy bodies rewarded me with their excitement. I allowed the canines to lead me wherever they desired as we strolled through the neighborhood.

I took a deep breath as fresh scents of nature promised a lovely spring. Even with the worst winters there was always something better waiting up ahead. That one winter had forever scarred me in a way that was irreversible. There would never be any way to escape the painful memories that plagued my dreams on the darkest of nights.

I had always been a strong believer in fate and destiny, but whenever I thought back on those awful days, it was hard to retain those views. I tried to convince myself there was a purpose for it all, but it was hard. I tried to pride myself on the thought that my influence had stopped a man, who could have easily become a mass murderer, but I knew that wasn't entirely true. Deep down, I understood that his death had not been to free me, He had killed himself to be free *of* me. I could see the way he changed in my presence. It was not my humanity he had attempted to preserve. The only thing he had been saved from was his own evil. From Cain.

Inhaling deeply, I pleaded with my mind for quiet. My thoughts had never been fully silent since my horrific experience. I blinked against the morbid images floating through my head. In time, the allure of such bloodshed had grown. My sense of humanity vehemently refuted such brutality, yet something felt amiss. It appeared the evils of my past refused to remain elusive.

Sylas assumed his death would eliminate his darkest side forever. What

he hadn't accounted for, was the fact that Cain wasn't gone. Not entirely. If the echo at the back of my head was any indication, it wouldn't be too long before he found his place in the world again. And if that entity returned, not even God himself would be able to stop it.

Lord help the next victims because he will be back. See you soon, Piper.

About the Author

A true nerd at heart, Nicki Lynn is a science- and math-lete and loves the academic rigor of school. Socially quirky, she has found it best to explore her ideas through written craft. When she is not whittling away at a new writing project or procrastinating on her homework, she is spending time with either her friends or her many pets (2 dogs and 3 cats). Although growing up in Charlotte, North Carolina, Nicki is a true northerner with a love of snow and busy cities.